GHOST
MUSIC

ALSO BY AN YU

Braised Pork

AN YU

GHOST

MUSIC

A NOVEL

Grove Press
New York

First published in 2022 in Great Britain by Harvill Secker,
an imprint of Vintage/Penguin Random House UK.

Published simultaneously in Canada
Printed in the United States of America

First Grove Atlantic hardcover edition: January 2023

Library of Congress Cataloging-in-Publication data is available for this title.

ISBN 978-0-8021-5962-5
eISBN 978-0-8021-5963-2

Grove Press
an imprint of Grove Atlantic
154 West 14th Street
New York, NY 10011

Distributed by Publishers Group West

groveatlantic.com

23 24 25 26   10 9 8 7 6 5 4 3 2 1

The more you know them, the less sure you feel about identifying them. Each one is itself. Each mushroom is what it is – its own centre.

John Cage, *For the Birds*

GHOST MUSIC

NIGHT

When I woke, the room was so black that I had to blink a few times to make sure my eyelids were really open. I stared through the deep black at what I believed to be the ceiling, taking extended breaths, waiting for my vision to adjust. Minutes passed, and still I was unable to make out any of the objects in the room. I must gradually have fallen asleep again, until I was woken a second time by a weak, squeaking voice.

'Excuse me, is anybody there? I would very much appreciate some help.'

I sat up and directed my attention to where the voice was coming from and saw a soft orange light near the floor. I quickly got out of bed, made my way over to it and squatted down to take a better look. A small mushroom – about the length of a hairpin – had sprouted from the boards. It had a thin stem, which supported its large, flat and slightly wrinkled cap. The top half of it was glowing, but the light hadn't made any of its surroundings visible. I prodded its cap with my index finger.

'I would rather not be touched,' the mushroom said.

I was certain that this was a dream. I brought my hand up to my nose and noticed a faint, musky smell at the tip of my finger.

'Can you please help me?' it said again.

'What do you need?' I asked.

'Well, you see, I'd like to be remembered.'

I looked around. Everything besides the mushroom was buried in darkness. This was unusual, as my mother-in-law always kept a light on in the living room for when she had to use the bathroom at night. I wasn't in our apartment; that was for sure. Wherever I was, it must have been an old place. There were smells of smoke and cooking oil that had been absorbed into the walls.

'It is normal that you don't understand,' the mushroom said, upon seeing how puzzled I was. Even though I would be mad to imagine it had eyes, I sensed it staring at me.

'But when you leave this room,' it said, 'I'd like you to remember me.'

All I could think of was finding a way to wake up. The air had already been moist, but the humidity had built even more in the past few minutes. I pinched myself on the forearm.

'I'm afraid that won't work,' the mushroom said. 'You're not in a dream. Not exactly.'

'If this isn't a dream,' I said, 'then how is it possible that I'm here, in this dark room, talking to a mushroom?'

'I am not a mushroom. Not in the way you think I am. And I cannot perceive light and darkness, unfortunately.'

'But you can perceive dream and reality?'

'You could say that. But oftentimes those two things are not so different.'

I stood up. Dream or reality, I had to leave the room. 'How do I get out of here?' I asked.

'I suggest you go back to bed, climb beneath the covers, make yourself comfortable and go to sleep. There is no other door out of this room.'

I wasn't convinced, and decided to prove the mushroom wrong. I placed my hands on the wall in front of me. It was a corner. I started moving to my left. The bricks were exposed; I could feel the mortar joints. After seven steps, I reached another corner, so I turned and continued. Seven more steps until the next corner. The whole time, I kept my eye fixed on the orange light so that I wouldn't lose my sense of direction. The third wall measured the same length, and examining the fourth, I discovered that I was in a square-shaped room, without a single door.

I had no choice but to trust the mushroom. The bed must be in the centre of the room, I reasoned, so I fumbled around for it in the dark, careful not to run my leg into its corners. I found it easily, and did as I was told.

To my surprise, it didn't take long for me to fall asleep. The orange mushroom said nothing more.

When I woke again, I was alone on my bed, the morning sky was a washed-out blue and in the corner of the room sat nothing but my dragon tree in its pot. To make sure, I dragged the pot to the side and checked the floors. No mushroom in sight. Relieved, I looked at the clock. It was a little before seven in the morning. I decided not to linger in bed and started my usual routine: I brewed a pot of oolong tea, put on the first movement of Schubert's Piano Sonata in B-flat major and took out the sheet music to follow along.

It was not until later, after the sonata had ended and I was stepping into the shower, that I noticed the musky smell on my finger.

DELIVERIES

My mother-in-law sat on the only stool in the apartment, fanning herself in the corner of the living room. The fan emitted a sandalwood scent as she waved it with one hand, her other hand clenched into a fist, drumming the pressure points on her legs. I was mopping the floor so that we could walk around in our socks, and Bowen had just found a knife and was cutting the plastic that was wrapped over the sofa. If it had been up to me, we would have moved into the new apartment in the autumn, during cooler weather, but my mother-in-law had begun to show signs of depression after Bowen's father had passed away the month before. During the day, I was told, she would lie in bed, only having enough energy to get up to use the toilet. She would cook one large pot of congee every Monday and eat it for the rest of the week. At night, she had started taking pills to fall asleep.

Bowen was a good son, and it was only to be expected that he couldn't allow his mother to be alone back in

Yunnan, so he had sold our old apartment and quickly purchased a larger one. He then brought his mother to Beijing, and that was how we were unpacking boxes while eating watermelon on a thirty-some-degrees day, preparing to live with my mother-in-law for the rest of the time she had in this world. She was still quite young, so I'd say at least twenty more years. If we took good care of her, perhaps she could live for another thirty.

When the doorbell rang, I was feeling thirsty and had just picked up a piece of melon from the plate on the piano bench. Bowen gestured to me to get the door. It was the delivery man, who handed me a box. It felt cold on the outside.

'Be sure to put it in the fridge as soon as possible,' he said. 'It's fresh produce.'

We had not informed anyone of our new address yet, not that we wanted to keep it secret, but the past few days had been too hectic. As the delivery man rushed off to his next address, Bowen was already urging me to make the bed for his mother, so I left the box on the floor and hurried to attend to her needs.

I found her in the bedroom already, unpacking her own duvet and sheets. She was sitting on the bed, try-ing to pull the plastic zip tie open with her hands.

'Ma,' I said, 'you're going to hurt yourself. Let me get you a pair of scissors.'

I went to get the toolbox from Bowen. It still felt strange to me, calling somebody I hardly knew 'Ma'.

Truth be told, I wasn't all that close with my own mother any more. Even before I married, I'd visited my parents no more than two or three times a year.

'Oh, thank you. I just didn't want to bother Bowen,' my mother-in-law explained, slightly embarrassed, when I came back with the scissors. 'He seemed busy with the sofa.'

I took over and began to make her bed while she stood tensely next to the door, watching me.

'Do you think these sheets are clean?' she asked while scratching the back of her ear with the tip of the fan.

'Well, they're new, although probably not as clean as we'd want them to be. But it doesn't seem like the washing machine will be arriving today.'

'That's too bad,' she said. 'I've just always cleaned everything before use. It must be a habit I picked up from my husband. He was quite adamant about that.'

I felt uncomfortable responding to anything related to Bowen's father, as Bowen had explicitly told me not to mention him in front of his mother. I nodded without looking back at her and continued to arrange the duvet cover.

'He was a very clean person,' she continued, oblivious to my unease. 'Always washing vegetables at least three times before cooking them. Cleaning the sheets every four days. Now, tell me, what was all that for? Did it keep him healthy?'

I was desperate to finish up so that I could join my husband in the living room. I had never been particularly skilful at comforting people, or speaking about those who were gone in a way that didn't feel overly disconnected. It wasn't because I couldn't feel sympathy for those who were mourning, more that in the face of such pain and loss, I always felt unworthy to offer anything.

Perhaps, I reasoned, my mother-in-law wasn't expecting a response anyway. The way her voice sounded, she could've been talking to a plant. As long as she could still speak about Bowen's father, it didn't matter to her whether anybody was listening. So I let her continue.

'Song Yan,' she said, 'I'm afraid that I will die soon too, just like my husband. I could also have a heart attack. And I wouldn't even be able to see my grandchildren.'

'Don't say such things. We'll take good care of you.'

'Are you and Bowen planning to have children soon?' She began fidgeting with the loose wardrobe door handles.

'He's quite focused on his job right now.'

I arranged the duvet and pillows and went for the door. My mother-in-law didn't say anything, but I heard her sigh when I walked out of the room. I hadn't met her many times before she moved to Beijing, but in the past few days I'd begun to piece together her personality. She had an air of sullenness, often sighing, never requesting anything outright, but making demands nonetheless. When she ran into an acquaintance on the street, she would give a smile that wouldn't linger beyond the moment she turned her head away. The way she asked for things often left others without room to say no: take, for instance, her move to Beijing. Although it was Bowen who had insisted, it was, certainly, her idea at first. She had refused to hire a caretaker, but continued to call her son every night to remind him of her inability to look after herself.

She was a polite lady, that much I did recognise. But the more well mannered she was, the more I sensed her disregard for my will.

Bowen and I had been married for three years. I'd wanted a child at first, but he'd been working to get a promotion at his company, so I had put off raising it with him. As time went by, I'd convinced myself that I could always afford to wait a few more years. As long as I had a child before I turned thirty-three, I was fine. But now that his mother had brought it up with me, I thought I could try and approach the topic.

'We've been married for three years,' I said that night, while combing my hair in the bathroom.

'Has it been three years already?' Bowen was sitting on the bed in his white undershirt, leaning against the headboard and reading printed PowerPoint slides.

He looked tired. He'd just gotten a fresh haircut and the barber had trimmed it to be unnaturally sharp and tidy, which didn't match his face at all. It sat stiffly on top of his head like a wig.

'I know that you're busy,' I said. 'But now that your mother is here, you know, we can probably start thinking about having a child.'

'She's your mother now too, Song Yan.' He sleeved the slides and sighed. He sighed in the same way as his mother, I noticed. A long inhale, followed by a short exhale.

'I'm still not used to that.' I turned off the bathroom light and sat on the bed, facing him. 'But Ma can help us take care of a child.'

'Did she say something to you?'

I nodded. 'She mentioned it. I also thought of it the other day, when I was teaching Yuyu. Her mother is pregnant again. With a boy, this time.'

He leaned towards me and picked an eyelash off my cheek. 'You just took on a new pupil, didn't you? And I, well, I hardly even have any time for you these days.'

Then he smiled and paused for a moment, just long enough for his words to sound sincere, and turned off the lamp.

The following day, I didn't have a lesson until the afternoon. I spent the morning chatting with my mother-in-law while scrubbing the kitchen sink.

'I finally slept well last night, without any medication,' my mother-in-law said through a yawn. 'In fact, I could barely wake up this morning. It must be because of all the oxygen here.'

'The oxygen?'

'The oxygen, for sure. Reverse altitude sickness is what they call it. I've spent my whole life in the highlands. There's too much oxygen here for me.'

'Now that you mention it, last time Bowen and I returned from Yunnan, I felt drowsy for days. I thought I was just tired from the travel.'

I rinsed the sponge and took off my rubber gloves.

'I heard that the temperatures are so comfortable there, it always feels like spring,' I said. 'When Bowen has more time, I want to do a road trip around Yunnan. We could fly into Kunming and drive up all the way to Shangri-La. What do you think?'

'Where are the cups?' My mother-in-law stood up from her stool. 'I want some water. It's so dry here, I'll never get used to it.'

I washed my hands and poured her a cup of warm water. I wondered if she knew that it was the wettest it ever gets in Beijing, with frequent summer rains and high levels of humidity in the air.

It was then that I remembered the package we'd received the day before. I found it still there by the door, where I had left it.

'What's that?' my mother-in-law asked when I brought the box over.

'I think it was delivered to the wrong address. We didn't order anything. Must be for the previous tenants.'

'Let's see what's inside.'

She took the box from me and began running a scissor blade through the tape, even though it was clear that she wasn't the one who had ordered it either. She'd finally expressed interest in something and I didn't want to overstep by telling her what not to do, so I let her open the package.

Inside the box were bags of mushrooms, a type I had never seen before. The ice packs had melted overnight.

'Ji zong mushrooms!' my mother-in-law cried out.

'What?' I asked, rather startled. She was the most excited I had ever seen her.

'Ji zong mushrooms. They're wild, grown in Yunnan. Did Bowen buy these?'

I examined the mushrooms. They looked appalling – a dirty brown, with long, overly thick stems and small, flaccid caps.

'I'll put them in the fridge for now and tell the delivery man to come get them,' I said.

'They'll spoil before then!' She shielded the box with her body. 'Why didn't you put these in the fridge last night? Thankfully, they still look really fresh. Bowen loved these when he was a child. Don't you know that Yunnan's mushrooms are famous around the country? It's not easy to get them outside of the province, especially ones that are fresh like these. We could make a soup for dinner tonight.'

Honestly, I couldn't agree with my mother-in-law on how fresh they looked. I had seen very few things in my life that looked less appetising. I still wanted to send them back, but my mother-in-law had begun to take them out of the box, feeling no guilt, it seemed, at keeping somebody else's package and already overly attached to this boxed-up reminder of her home. The sight of the mushrooms had woken her from her doldrums.

'I'll teach you how to cook these,' she said with a proud smile, rolling up her sleeves. 'Bowen will be so happy.'

'Ma, I have to go out. I have a lesson. I'll be back before dinner.'

'Don't come home too late. Can you buy a chicken while you're out?'

I agreed, because I didn't want to argue with her. I changed my clothes and left the apartment.

This was my first lesson with little Shaobo, and it took me almost an hour to find where he lived, though it was not far from us, in an old brick building. As far as I knew, little Shaobo did not have a mother; perhaps his parents were divorced, or something had happened to her, but it was not my place to ask. His father's apartment was crowded with furniture and all kinds of objects: toys, bowls, newspapers, snacks, a Go board, paintbrushes and all sorts of other things. They even had a red and black war bonnet, which little Shaobo put on his head and wore for the entire lesson. The air conditioning was off and though the windows were open, the air was still and stale.

Little Shaobo was six years old, and his father had decided that he wanted his son to learn an instrument, reasoning that once little Shaobo was old enough for university, skill at the piano would give him a better chance at being admitted to a top-tier school. I thought about telling him that it was not so simple, that most children would find it impossible to achieve the level of expertise required. If he wanted little Shaobo to go to a top-tier university, using the extra time to study would probably be more effective. Many of my students' parents had similar aspirations, and each time I heard about them, I felt grateful that my own father never saw the piano as a means for me to achieve something else. As a concert pianist himself, the piano is the beginning, middle and end for my father. University, relationships, even his career – they are simply there as support for his artistic pursuit. He is a pure and simple man. I admire him for it. I know how difficult it is; after all, I've failed to live like that.

I fished out *John Thompson's Easiest Piano Course* books from my tote. Little Shaobo had such small hands that he had to stretch to place his fingers on five adjacent keys. The war bonnet was too big and kept falling over his eyes. It also made him sweat, but when

I asked him whether he wanted to take it off, he held it in place and wouldn't let go.

Before we began, I told little Shaobo what I told all my students: 'The one thing more important than playing the piano is listening to yourself play.'

Though he nodded, he did not understand what I was trying to say, and I didn't blame him. Still, they were words that I wish my teacher had said to me at the beginning, when I was a child touching those black and white keys for the first time. It was not until I was at university that someone pointed out that I had not been listening to myself.

'What do you mean?' I had asked Dong Mo, the older student, at the time.

'You're not listening,' she'd said. 'So how do you know what you're playing?'

I realised then how much more difficult it is to change behaviour developed through the years than it is to adopt an entirely new one. Perhaps that was why I never became a concert pianist and settled for being a teacher instead.

Little Shaobo expressed a strong level of interest for the first fifteen minutes or so, but then, abruptly, as if possessed by a spirit, he jumped up from his seat and started putting on his quad skates. No matter what his father said, he would not touch the piano again, so I ended the lesson early, assuring his father that this was common in my experience of teaching children and there was nothing he should apologise for.

As requested by my mother-in-law, I picked up a whole chicken, and headed home in time for dinner preparations.

'The key to cooking mushrooms is not to do too much with them,' my mother-in-law explained to me while she started chopping. 'Call Bowen to see when he's coming back.'

'I'll send him a text. He's still at work.'

My mother-in-law's fingers were long and slender, though her stature was small and plump. Her fingernails were cut short like mine. She had age spots on the backs of her hands that stretched to her forearms. It was as though each of them held a little story beneath the thinning skin. There was something alluring about an aging woman's hands, I thought, weary but resilient, weathered by the experiences of her years, by everything she had touched. They were a book without words.

Bowen came back a little after eight. We added the ji zong mushrooms to the chicken soup and waited another half an hour before serving the dish. I could tell that Bowen must have been bothered by something that had happened during the day – he did not speak much and he shook his head every once and again at nothing in particular.

'Son,' my mother-in-law said to him as I carried the pot of soup to the table, 'someone mailed us some ji zong mushrooms yesterday. We made a pot of soup with half of them, so we'll have enough for tomorrow too. You look like you've lost weight. You ought to eat more.'

'Who gave us these?' Bowen asked while I fished out a few pieces of chicken and served them along with some soup for my mother-in-law. She took the bowl over and handed it to Bowen.

'I don't think they were meant for us,' I said. 'The box was addressed to somebody else.' I immediately regretted saying so, aware that I must have irritated my mother-in-law.

'Don't worry about it, son,' she said, ignoring me. 'Try it.'

Bowen liked the soup; he ate at least half the pot. It tasted much better than I had initially presumed. The mushrooms had a silky texture to them, and a delicate, earthy aroma. They tasted a little like chicken.

'Do you remember when you were young, we used to go pick mushrooms with your father?' my mother-in-law said.

Bowen forced a smile. 'You have to eat some too, Ma.'

'I'll eat, I'll eat. I'm not hungry yet.' She watched him start his third bowl. 'Do you remember when you ate some mushrooms and had to be sent to the hospital? I think you were about ten or eleven. Turned out you

were allergic. We still don't know what kind of mushroom it was.'

'Ma, I know. You've told me many times.'

'And remember your second uncle? He died from
accidentally eating a death cap.'

'Death cap?' I asked. 'What do those look like?'

'They're white,' my mother-in-law said to me.
'There's nothing special about their appearance. But
they're deadly poisonous.'

When I was a child, my father told me that only colour-
ful mushrooms are poisonous. And as with many things
a parent tells their children, it never occurred to me that
he could be wrong; it became a fact to me, etched into my
memory like a natural law of this world.

I was listening intently to my mother-in-law recall-
ing all the mushroom incidents from Bowen's childhood
when I heard a thump. When I looked down, Bowen's
bowl was rolling on the tabletop. The soup had spilled
and stained the cloth, and Bowen was storming into
the bedroom.

I couldn't decide whether to follow my husband or
stay at the table and finish dinner with my mother-in-
law, so I just sat there shifting my glance between the
pot of soup in the middle of the table and the spilled
bowl that Bowen had left behind.

My mother-in-law forced a cough, either trying to
break the silence or signalling for me to go check on
Bowen – I couldn't tell. I got up and tiptoed into the

bedroom. Bowen was sitting on the bed, smoking and reading the same PowerPoint slides from last night.

'What's wrong?' I asked.

He ignored me. His eyes were squinting from the smoke that was rising from the cigarette in his mouth.

When he realised that I wouldn't leave until he gave me an answer, he said, 'How was your lesson today? New student?'

'Yes. A boy.'

'Big hands?'

'No.'

He let out a short 'hmm' and then went back to his reading. I was afraid to probe further, so I closed the door and went back to the dining table. My mother-in-law was spitting out some chicken bones onto her plate. She didn't ask me about Bowen; instead, she gestured for me to sit down. It was a hot, oppressive evening, as if the air was holding its breath in anticipation of a night of strong storms ahead. My mother-in-law and I sat in silence: I thought it important to let her eat in peace. I counted the bits of chicken she ate and the bones she spat out, and on her eleventh bone, she finally spoke.

'I have a daughter,' she said. 'But we were so poor, we had to give her away when she was three years old. Her name is Boyan. Yan as in "swallows". Now that I think about it, it's the same Yan as the one in your name.'

This was the first time I had heard that Bowen had a sister. We dated for two years before getting married, and he had always told me that he was an only child. How could he have kept this from me for all those years? Why would he do that?

'Is she older than Bowen?' I asked.

'Bowen is the older one. Even though it was a short three years, they were very close. As Bowen grew up, he gradually spoke less about Boyan, and nowadays he pretends like she never existed.' She put her chopsticks down and leaned back into her chair.

I wasn't sure what to feel: anger or sympathy. I convinced myself that the reason Bowen hadn't told me was because he was unable to articulate losing someone as close to him as his sister, yet in this reassurance I suddenly felt selfish, as though I had put myself at the centre of his trauma.

'Do you know where she is?' I asked, trying to direct my mind towards the abandoned girl.

'Back then, I decided I didn't want to know, otherwise I'd go after her. But ever since Bowen's father died, she keeps coming back to me in my dreams. On days like this one, I feel like Bowen still hasn't forgiven me one bit.'

Once again, I was at a loss as to what to say. Before I knew it, I had put my hand on hers. They were firm and cold, slightly oily from the chicken, and they were clenched tightly together.

'Looks like it's going to rain soon,' she said, her voice raspy.

Later that night, before going to bed, I took out the rubbish. The rain hadn't started yet, but I could hear muted moans of thunder in the distance. I looked at the empty mushroom box in my hand and read the half-torn piece of paper stuck on the lid.

Sender: Bai Yu

Ship to: Ms Tian

My father's favourite contemporary pianist was also named Bai Yu. Even the characters were the same, meaning 'white feather'. Bai Yu the pianist was a prodigy. My father had often told me to play like him – to forget about my own emotions and stay faithful to the composer's intentions. But no matter how hard I tried, I'd never been able to do it right. When I became older, I understood that it was because I heard something different in Bai Yu's playing. He was undoubtedly a brilliant pianist – his performance was as light and pure as his name – but it had always aroused a crushing fear in me, as if the countless layers of perfection hid a bottomless hole, and in the hole there was something as heavy as the world.

Bai Yu's most famous moment, though, came after he disappeared. I was still at university. There was a thunderstorm that day, which must've been after one of my father's recitals. Water dripped from his tailcoat as he came through the door with a soggy newspaper inside his leather bag. Sitting on the sofa, he read the article about the missing pianist to us while my mother wiped his hair with a towel.

A few weeks after Bai Yu disappeared, the authorities were still unable to find him. As time passed, people started to forget about the piano prodigy, until a short post by a blogger expressed concern that Bai Yu might have died. The post picked up some steam, and for a few days 'Is Bai Yu Dead?' was among the top searches across the internet. People who didn't know anything about classical music were suddenly watching his videos and keeping up with the story, but nobody ever found out what happened to him. He was neither alive nor dead, simply gone.

I read the shipping label again. There wasn't a return address or a phone number I could call, so I threw away the box and went back inside.

The next morning, Bowen was packing his briefcase when I decided to bring up the idea of children again. It was not for my mother-in-law, I told myself, it was for me, for us. I had not slept a wink, the mists of Bowen's past swirling in my mind as I thought about how he had never revealed much at all about the years before he moved to Beijing. It was as if I had only known half the man who was my husband. I'd tried to question him a little on his childhood before, and had been satisfied with his short answers at the time, but now that I knew about Boyan, things were different.

'I've thought it over,' I said. 'I do want to have a child.'

'I don't have time right now. It's raining. The traffic is probably horrible.'

He was still visibly upset from whatever had been troubling him at dinner the previous night, but I pushed further. My determination was like a weed that sprouts up one morning, entirely unforeseen.

'If you just agree, it won't be a long conversation,' I told him, as assertively as I could. 'And then you can run off to work as quick as you like.'

'Why are you in such a rush all of a sudden?' He stuffed his phone into his briefcase and tried to leave the room. I got to the door before him and planted myself in front of it, blocking his way.

I held up three fingers. 'I'm going to be thirty next year.'

He looked taller than usual. Seeing that I refused to move, he eventually sat down on the chair next to the door with his briefcase on his lap. We stayed in those positions for a while.

'I won't have any time for the child,' he muttered.

'You'll make time. Who knows what will happen in two or three years? You might be even busier than you are now, especially if you get that promotion. I gave up on becoming a concert pianist for the sake of this family.'

'You had given up on that long before you met me.'

I opened my mouth to speak but couldn't find any words. He got up and left, leaving me standing in the bedroom. He didn't even have breakfast.

After I brushed my teeth and cleaned myself up, I saw that my mother-in-law was in the living room, focusing on some embroidery work on a handkerchief. She told me that she was stitching a red-crowned crane with a background of peonies. I left her alone, put on some Chopin nocturnes, and spent the whole morning on my computer buying books on how to have a healthy conception and pregnancy. I avoided thinking about an alternate life; the life I had always trusted I would lead, where mornings like these would be spent on practising, on becoming better.

Growing up, I had been told to focus solely on playing the piano, just like my father had, and everything else to be done around the house was left to my mother. I had no reason to be unsuccessful, as I had dedicated all my waking hours to refining one skill. And as time went by and I improved, the only choice I faced was to become even better. But the more I practised, the clearer it became that there was going to come a point where I wouldn't be able to improve any more. *What would happen after that?* I started asking myself. I began to realise that for most people, talent had a limit that couldn't be surpassed.

With every passing day I found it harder to find purpose in persisting. Until one afternoon, a few days before graduating from university, in a final moment of crisis, I gave it all up and was left with nothing but a pair of hands that could translate notes into sounds.

For the first few months afterwards, I thought I had finally begun to live. I spent time with friends, travelled to Japan and Malaysia, indulged in TV. I watched the piano collect dust. I avoided going home to meet my father's rage, and passed messages through my devastated mother. She was afraid, she told me on the phone, that I didn't know how to do anything else, that I was too old to choose another path, that I would be able to find no other purpose in life. Later, when I learned that she was right, I had already allowed my decision to become permanent. I locked myself up at home and sat in front of the piano for days, but every sound came out worse than the one before – mediocre, rushed, broken. I had, for the first time, deteriorated. I had a single chance, I came to conclude, one that did not allow room for my instability, one that hung on a thread. And so, in my vacant drift, I met Bowen and gave my life to him.

It wasn't until we started dating that I learned how to cook. I stopped caring about cutting my fingers or burning my hands. Steadily, as I found some comfort and air in this other way of living, of caring for

someone else, I thought that I didn't want to be like my
father after all.

After I bought the books, I ate Bowen's bowl of noodles
along with an egg. I had no appetite, but reasoning that
I must keep a strong body for my eventual pregnancy, I
forced myself to eat it all. I immediately felt nauseous,
and for the next hour I lay flat on the sofa until my student arrived for her lesson.

Yuyu and her mother wore matching outfits: a red
raincoat over a light blue dress. Her mother's belly was
bulging out a little under the linen fabric.

'Say "Hello, Ms Song".' Yuyu's mother tapped her
daughter on the back of her head.

'Hello, Ms Song,' the girl repeated in a whisper. She
had been my student for over two years, but her shy-
ness had not reduced a bit. She would rarely speak, and
only gave a small nod when I said something. I was
very much the same way as a teenager. But the other
part of Yuyu, the part I was more curious about, bore
no resemblance to myself. When she played the piano,
her performance was, from the very first day, so full of
confidence and vigour that I often wondered whether
there was another person hiding within her.

While Yuyu sat at the piano going through warm-up
exercises, my mother-in-law moved into her bedroom
to continue her embroidery. I poured Yuyu's mother
and myself some apple juice and we sat at the coffee

table. We always started the lesson like this – Yuyu warming up for five minutes while her mother and I chatted.

'I'm sorry my new apartment is further away from you,' I said. 'Now that you're pregnant, it must take a lot to come all the way here. I'll try to go to yours more often.'

'Some exercise is good for me,' she said with a forgiving smile. Her voice was very similar to that of her daughter – they both spoke in hushed tones. To understand her over the sound of the piano, I had to read her lips.

'My husband and I are thinking about having a child too,' I told her.

I enjoyed the sound of those words. They gave me a sense of reassurance, as if now that I had voiced them out loud, they had become a fact, rather than just an idea. There was a wholeness that was embedded in that sentence, as if Bowen and I were one and the same, and for a brief second I thought I could allow the part of him that was unknown to me to remain buried in the past.

'Really? What wonderful news!' Yuyu's mother said, her eyes widening.

'Soon I'll have to consult you about pregnancy precautions.'

'Of course, Ms Song. Of course. It would be my pleasure.' She picked up her glass of juice, looked at it with the fascination of a jeweller observing a rare stone, and took a sip.

'All right!' I said to Yuyu. 'Let's begin.'

Yuyu was going to take her Grade 7 exam the next day. She didn't seem as anxious as I'd imagined she'd be.

'Why don't we do a mock exam,' I told her.

She nodded.

'Very well. I'd like you to play the B-flat major and its relative minor scale.'

She did as she was told and breezed through the scales and arpeggios.

I tuned my voice down to give her some pressure.

'You may start your pieces.'

I had no criticisms for her Czerny étude, so like an examiner would do, I cut her off halfway through and asked her to continue with the courante from Bach's French Suite in C minor. When Yuyu first started having lessons with me, she'd let the same emotions saturate every piece she played. They all sounded like snippets from a victory dance – triumphant, animated, bustling with happiness. Throughout the past two years, her music had become more mature and nuanced, but more often than not those feelings of celebration came through just as strongly as before. They were in the details now – she revelled in all the rubatos and fermatas and honoured them as though each one was a miracle.

I let her perform the rest of the pieces in full. After

the last one, Tchaikovsky's 'June (Barcarolle)' from *The Seasons*, she looked up at me.

'You're still rushing through the courante,' I said. 'Keep the rhythm in your heart nice and steady. Pay more attention to the melody in your left hand, stick to it, and try not to get carried away by your right.'

'Do you think she'll be all right tomorrow?' her mother asked from the couch.

'She'll do well.' I smiled and put my hand on Yuyu's shoulder. 'I think we can aim to get a Distinction.'

I sat down next to Yuyu and told her, 'You know, Tchaikovsky didn't put much effort into composing *The Seasons* because he was so busy with *Swan Lake*, but you make "June" sound like it's the most important piece ever written.'

'Oh!' her mother said with a big smile and started clapping. 'Hurry up, Yuyu, thank Ms Song!'

'Thank you, Ms Song,' Yuyu said.

I patted her back and said, 'Let's go through the courante again.'

When Bowen came home that night, he was with two of his colleagues. Under the supervision of my mother-in-law, I stir-fried the rest of the mushrooms, and the dish received much praise from our guests. After dinner, we sat around the table, drinking tea.

'You've settled in so quickly!' Wang Xiao said. Like Bowen, he had been working at BMW for the entirety of his professional life. He had started in the Shanghai office, but requested to be transferred when he got married to Ruya, who was from Beijing.

'It's all thanks to the women here,' Bowen said. 'You know how I'm at the office all the time.'

I had always been rather fond of Wang Xiao and Ruya. We used to live in the same compound. When Bowen went on business trips, Wang Xiao would make sure to take care of me. He would stop by on his way back from work to drop off fruit that he had picked up at the supermarket. He was a classical music enthusiast, so whenever he came he'd politely request that I play a few pieces for him. Sometimes, when her husband was too busy, Ruya would come in his place, and we'd gossip over coffee and whatever dessert she brought with her that day. From the way she spoke, she seemed to have countless groups of friends. She knew so many people that I think if I wanted to meet with the mayor of, say, Shijiazhuang, she'd probably be able to make it happen. She'd brought me to a few of her gatherings before. Once, she even invited me to her grandfather's mahjong group, where she chatted and drank baijiu with his friends as though they were her own. It was only afterwards that she told me she didn't know most of them. I could never fathom how people were able to adapt themselves to fit into the lives of so many others, so I found her extraordinary in that way.

Those kindnesses were not the only reasons I enjoyed

Wang Xiao and Ruya's company so much. There was a quiet harmony between them, something that I couldn't quite describe. Whatever it was, it was something that Bowen and I didn't have. They were like water in two streams that had merged and then separated again. And even if they now diverged, flowing through different terrains, taking on various shapes, they had once been one and the same, and who could possibly remove them from each other? I found that refreshing.

'I heard from Bowen that you're a pianist, Ms Song,' Mr Lu said to me. He was one of Bowen's younger colleagues, and this was my first time meeting him. He was bald-headed, which made his thick-rimmed glasses stand out.

'I'm a piano teacher,' I responded.

'Do you have any recitals coming up? I'd love to see you play.' He had a big smile on his face.

'Well, I only teach these days.'

'Stop pretending,' Bowen said to Mr Lu, laughing. 'You strike me as the kind of guy who'd fall asleep at a piano recital.'

Wang Xiao nodded. 'I have to agree with Bowen.'

'I can't deny that,' Mr Lu said. 'But I wouldn't dare to fall asleep at Ms Song's recital! Bowen, do you also play the piano?'

'I could never,' Bowen responded without giving it more than a second of thought. 'I know next to nothing about music.'

'That's too bad,' Wang Xiao said. 'As a child, I would make sure to have my Walkman with me at all times. I even slept with music on.'

'I was the same!' Mr Lu said. 'But I have to admit, I didn't listen to classical music.'

'Wang Xiao,' I said, changing the subject, 'how's your wife these days? I haven't seen her in quite a long time.'

'She's travelling with her friends. Oh!' Wang Xiao slapped himself on the side of his head. 'How could I forget! Bowen, where in Yunnan are you from? My wife is there right now.'

'I'm pretty much from Beijing now,' Bowen responded. 'I was born in Chuxiong, not far from Kunming.'

'I should've told her to ask you about Yunnan before she went,' Wang Xiao said, still tapping his head. 'There's no point now. She's coming back tomorrow.'

'Tell her to come see our new place,' I said.

'Of course, we'll come together.'

I noticed that my mother-in-law had stayed rather quiet throughout the meal. The only sounds she made came from sipping her tea. I remembered that she hadn't eaten much at dinner so I went into the kitchen and washed some cherries. When I returned, Bowen's colleagues were standing up, saying their goodbyes.

After they left, my mother-in-law went into her room without saying a thing.

*

As always, Bowen fell asleep before me. I lay there for a while, listening to his breathing. Usually, I liked having this time to myself. I'd let my thoughts wander for a while until the rhythm of Bowen's breaths gradually led each thought back to its nest. But then, every so often, there would be nights like this one, when I'd feel lonelier than usual and wish that I could be the one to fall asleep being watched over by him.

At around three in the morning, I went into the living room and saw my mother-in-law sitting on her stool, looking out the window. She was fanning herself. The only light came from outside. With her back towards me, I couldn't see her face.

'Did I wake you?' she said without turning.

'Are you having trouble sleeping?'

'I'm thinking about her again,' she said. 'These days, the more I look at Bowen, the more I'm reminded of Boyan.'

I walked towards her and perched against the piano. From there, I could see only her profile.

'Would you want to find her again?' I asked.

She didn't give an answer. For a while, we watched the wind blow through the trees along the pavements.

'Can you bring me the cherries?' she said.

I went into the kitchen and fetched the bowl of cherries I'd washed.

'Have you ever thought about how the soil changes depending on where you are?' she said as I handed over the bowl. 'I mean, have you actually taken a moment to think about that? The colour, the texture, the rocks that are mixed in the soil, all that. And how much loneliness it brings you, looking out the window at unfamiliar soil?'

I wondered whether Boyan was still living in Yunnan, and if not, what kind of soil was she walking on now? We are all like trees, I thought, our heads swaying in the wind, our roots buried in the ground, unseen by anyone, and at times forgotten even by ourselves.

'What's the soil like in Yunnan?' I asked.

'Oh, where I'm from, it's red.'

'Red?'

'Yes, completely red.' With that, my mother-in-law stood up and walked towards her room, cherries in hand. 'Hopefully, eating something will help me fall asleep,' she said before lightly shutting the door behind her.

All I could hear now was the rhythm of my own finger tapping against the fallboard of the piano. The heavy rain hadn't stopped all day, as if trying to wash away traces of something. I looked outside and noticed a dimly lit apartment in the building across the street – another person who was awake in the darkest hours. I didn't know who it was, of course, and that didn't matter anyway. What brought me a touch of comfort was knowing not that my husband was there, asleep on the other side of the wall, but that there was a stranger, across the street, still awake and listening to the same rain.

The next day, I was on my way to a lesson when Ruya called and asked to meet. We agreed to see each other at a coffee shop in Wangjing. I headed there immediately I'd finished, found a table in the corner and ordered some black coffee. Two teenage boys took the table next to mine: one had a guitar case, the other was holding some drumsticks.

When Ruya sat down across from me, she had on white-rimmed sunglasses that were too large for her petite, diamond-shaped face. She had grown quite tanned since I last saw her.

'How was your flight?' I asked.

'Oh, let's not talk about it,' she said. 'The take-off was horrible. I've never been through such bad turbulence. After that I just couldn't relax. You must know how bad it is when you can't relax on a flight.' She leaned back in the leather chair. 'I just kept reminding myself that the first thing I was going to do when I landed was go to McDonald's and get a sundae. Live life, you know?'

I laughed.

'Look, you wouldn't be laughing if you had been on that flight,' she said.

'So, did you get your sundae?'

'Of course!' Now she laughed too. She took off her sunglasses and placed them on the table.

'Why didn't you go home and rest?' I asked.

'I have a dance lesson in a bit. Plus, I thought I'd come see how you are doing, now that your mother-in-law is here.'

'Well, we're slowly learning to live with each other.'

Inevitably, I'd been thinking about Boyan. I'd tried my best to act normally in front of Bowen, and after he went to work, I'd anticipated that my mother-in-law would bring up the subject of her daughter again, but she had just gone on with her routine. I could tell that she – like me – was a little more in her own space and less in ours that morning.

The waitress came with my coffee. The cup was too full and the coffee had overflowed onto the saucer before arriving at our table. The little biscuit next to the cup was soggy.

'Do you want to order something to drink?' I asked.

Ruya flipped through the menu that the waitress handed her and then asked for an iced tea. When the waitress left, Ruya leaned forward and started folding and unfolding her sunglasses.

'I'm quite torn about this, honestly,' she said. 'Normally, I hate to be the one gossiping behind others' backs, but it also doesn't feel right to keep this from you.'

In fact, this was far from the truth: she loved talking about others. Unlike her, I didn't find there to be anything wrong with that. Most people, whether they like to admit it or not, find pleasure in discussing things that are none of their business. Talking about people is fun. Talking about people without them knowing is thrilling. The way I see it, to be talked about is a natural – though bothersome – part of living as a person in this world.

'So what is it?' I said.

'I've known Bowen for seven or eight years now,' Ruya said. 'Still, I don't think I know him very well.'

I was surprised to hear that what she was about to say involved Bowen. I'd never heard anyone gossip about Bowen.

'He's a quiet man when it comes to his personal life, you know?' Ruya said. 'I know he tells us plenty of things about his family. But he never really talks about himself or how he *feels*.'

I chewed on the mushy biscuit while pondering her comment.

'So I'm married to a robot?' I asked, trying to lighten the mood with a joke.

She looked up at me with a concerned expression and shook her head.

'No, no, not that. I'm sorry. I didn't mean it that way. It's just that I wonder if he's the same way at home? I imagine he must be quite different with you.'

I couldn't agree with her immediately. Was Bowen more open with me? I was certainly able to tell how he felt, most of the time. But was it simply because I spent

more time with him? Had he ever revealed his feelings
to me willingly? I felt suddenly defensive and was about
to say something, but the waitress came back with the
iced tea. A lemon wedge was balanced on the rim. I
watched Ruya squeeze the juice into her drink and
wipe her hands with a napkin.

Seeing that I hadn't responded to her statement, she
must've assumed that Bowen was indeed different with
me. She took a sip of the tea and frowned. Perhaps it
was too tart, or too sweet.

'This really is none of my business, but I saw his ex-
wife recently,' she said.

I recalled, vividly, the day that Bowen told me I was
his second girlfriend. The first had been a girl he met in
secondary school, or so he said to me. Their relationship had lasted less than a year and could hardly be
considered a relationship at all. I remembered thinking
that it was strange for a thirty-two-year-old man to
have been single all these years. But I'd taken it as a sign
of devotion and dignity – traits that I'd believed to be
representative of a good man.

I wanted Ruya to say more, but I was embarrassed to
ask, since that would've given away the truth: that I
hadn't a clue about what she was saying.

'Where did you see her?' I said, trying my best to
sound casual.

'In Yunnan. She's a friend of Muyi. You know Muyi?'
I shook my head.

'She's one of the ladies I met at dance lessons. Remember? She has small eyes and hair that goes all the way down to her thighs.'

This time I nodded and pretended I remembered.

'We were all out at dinner one night with Muyi and her friends,' she said. 'Bowen's ex-wife was among them. I was telling the story about that time Bowen caught a huge grass carp on our fishing trip. When I mentioned his name, I saw this woman's face turn pale. I'm telling you, pale like the moon.'

She drank more of her tea and then pushed it aside. She continued:

'It looked so bad that I had to ask her if she was all right. She said she was fine, so I kept going with my story. Eventually, she just gave an excuse and left before finishing dinner. Muyi later found out from her that she'd been married to Bowen for four years and that he left her when he came to Beijing. How come I've never heard about this? Is it true?'

I wished I could've told her that it was all made-up, or that it was all true. Neither would've bothered me too much, I think, but the fact was I didn't know, and that made me want to say something hostile to Ruya – blame her for prying, for being so confrontational. I held myself back, knowing full well that none of this was her fault.

I took a deep breath and asked whether she'd found out the woman's name.

'Julia,' Ruya said.

'Julia?'

'I don't know her actual name. She goes by Julia.'

Ruya gazed into my eyes, waiting for a reaction. I had no words. This piece of news, even if it somehow turned out to be a misunderstanding, came like a match igniting a mound of firewood that had been piling up inside me since my mother-in-law had moved to Beijing, bringing with her everything that I didn't know about Bowen. It was as if Bowen's past had materialised into a sudden gust of wind, blowing him away from me in a matter of days. First Boyan, now Julia.

'This Julia probably got confused,' I said, defending my husband. 'Bowen is not exactly that unique a name.'

'That's what I think as well.' Ruya's lips widened into a smile.

She looked at her watch, took the straw out of her drink and gulped down the rest of the iced tea.

'I have to go to my dance lesson. I'll call you another time.'

She placed some money on the table, grabbed her sunglasses and left hurriedly.

I sat there alone with her empty glass and watched the people around me. It was as if my ears had been blocked; I couldn't hear a thing anyone was saying. I looked at their faces and thought about how curious a place a coffee shop was, how there were very few spaces where one could observe so many facets of human emotion yet at the same time feel utterly alone. What expression did I wear? I wondered. I stayed until I finished my coffee and the sounds had gradually come back to me.

When I got home, Bowen was already there, smoking, his legs up on his desk. My mother-in-law was busy with her embroidery. Looking at the two of them, I felt unnecessary, as if I had been inserted into a painting that would've been better without me.

'I'm back,' I said with a smile.

In that moment, I envied those women who could allow their emotions to blow up freely without fear of destroying the calmness of a quiet household at night. Ruya would've been able to do that. Perhaps she would've even thrown an object or two at her husband. Unlike me, she wouldn't have been afraid of being a capricious wife, and that, I realised, was why Wang Xiao loved her.

I avoided saying anything else to Bowen and went straight to the kitchen. He must've finally sensed that I had something on my mind because before we went to bed, while I was changing into my pyjamas, he came to touch me. Holding my hair up, he placed his lips on the back of my neck. I let him run his hands over my waist and my breasts, and when he lay me down on the bed and tried to reach into the bedside drawer, I stopped him.

'I want a child,' I said.

'What's the matter with you these days?' His voice was a low whisper. He withdrew his hand, and his breath blew against my shoulders as he moved his lips to my chest.

'What's wrong with wanting children?' I said, sitting up.

'Let's not talk about this now,' he said quietly, leaning in to kiss me while kneeling on the bed.

Close up, his face looked like a stranger's. His eyes, nose, lips and cheeks all seemed as if they had been taken out and arranged in slightly different positions. They looked like parts of a person I had never seen before. The only thing that seemed somewhat familiar was that new haircut of his. Without thinking, I pushed him away, with stronger force than I intended, throwing him off balance and making him stumble off the edge of the bed.

'You've lost your mind!' he yelled. He pushed himself up, snatched a pillow, swung open the door and marched out of the bedroom. I heard his mother ask him what was wrong. He didn't respond. Then she peered into our room, where I still sat on the bed, naked, looking at the empty space where Bowen had been not so long ago.

* * *

A few days later, we received another delivery of mushrooms. Again, it was sent from Bai Yu and addressed to Ms Tian, without a phone number or return address.

The only difference was that this time, inside the box, there was a bag of round, green mushrooms. I told the delivery man that the package wasn't meant for us. He looked at me as though he didn't understand, then he took the box from my hands, looked inside, frowned and left without saying anything.

The next day, while I was at little Shaobo's place, the delivery man brought the mushrooms back again. My mother-in-law told me later, while I was accompanying her on a walk around Ritan Park, that without a return address, they couldn't figure out where it was mailed from.

'It's like the mushrooms followed me to Beijing,' my mother-in-law said, laughing. 'The ones we received today are called qing tou mushrooms. Since they're green and small, they're not easy to spot on the forest floor, but if you find one, there's always another one within two steps.'

She guided me to a bench.

'My shoulders hurt. Let's rest a bit,' she said.

I waited for her to sit down and then asked carefully, 'Ma, why do you think Bowen never told me about his sister? I've been thinking these days that I really don't know much about his life before we met, and I'm not just talking about Boyan . . .'

I stopped. I might already have sounded too critical.

My mother-in-law gave a groan and started reaching her hand over her back. I took this as a sign she wanted

me to massage her, so I got up from the bench and circled behind her.

'Oh, I can do it myself,' she said.

'Don't worry about it,' I said as I placed my hands on
her shoulders.

She patted my hand with hers to show her gratitude.

'I'm really getting old,' she said. 'At my age, I find myself
forgetting a lot of things. The more I start to forget, the
louder those unforgettable memories grow. And then I
talk on and on about them. You know how they say that
time will heal all things? What I've learned is that time
does nothing more than make pain more permanent.'

She turned round and said, 'I never meant to get
between you and Bowen. Will you forgive me and just
think of what I said as an old story?'

'We're family, Ma. There's nothing to forgive.'

After walking her back to the apartment building, I
remained outside for a while. Before we moved to the
new place, I would often meander around Chaoyang
Park alone. Winters were the most pleasant. I would
buy a stick of candied hawthorn and munch on it while
I walked along the different paths. At that time of the
year, when the outside air was sharp and bitter and
people were huddled in their heated homes, the city
would at last feel balanced to me. Just bare enough, just
full enough.

*   *   *

Bowen slept in the living room for a week until my mother-in-law expressed her discontent with our arrangements. Her son had long work days, she explained to me, and he needed restful sleep, so I brought his pillow back into the bedroom one afternoon. That evening, he slept in our bed as if nothing had happened.

Those earlier nights I had spent mostly awake, door slightly ajar, listening to Bowen's snores drift into the bedroom. I had not known that it was possible for an apartment to feel at once so cramped and so empty. As I lay there, it was as though a giant rock had been dumped onto my chest. Solitude is tolerable, even enjoyable at times. But when you realise that you've given your life to someone, yet you know nothing but his name? That kind of solitude is loneliness. That's what kills you.

Days and weeks passed like ships in a port. I felt as if I had missed the moment to confront Bowen about his previous marriage. As my frustration changed from an explosion to a contained, drumming beat, I talked myself into believing everyone had secrets they wanted to keep, even from those closest to them. I told myself I should be understanding, but the truth was that I had never been able to look another person in the eye and interrogate them. Most people concerned themselves with what brought them joy, whether romantic, professional or familial, but I concerned myself entirely with avoiding shame. During childhood, whenever I felt the need to express my anger, I wasn't allowed to do anything but withdraw into silence and walk away. At the time, I'd believed that anger was the most selfish of emotions. Everybody would be better off without it.

The result was that I seemed happy to most people, even myself. There was an invisible quality to a person like me – a seemingly happy person. This is not to say that those who live with genuine happiness are the same – in fact, in my experience, they are the people who shine most brightly. But that was not the person I had moulded myself into.

After Bowen moved back into our room, I began focusing on the small, kind gestures that came from my husband. He brought some tea back from work, a present from his co-worker, and I threw myself at him and told him how caring he was. I asked him whether he'd be willing to pick up some garlic on his way home and when he did as I had asked, I was reassured by the thought that he must care at least a little about our home. Things like this distracted me, and I moved on, as I had always done, without any fuss.

I didn't mention another word about children to Bowen. I kept the idea in my own head and began taking notes on all those books I'd bought about pregnancy. I made up my mind to approach this patiently.

Instead, it was my mother-in-law who began building up resentment. She tried to hide it, but more often than not, she let her words betray her. Women in

Yunnan were more family-oriented, she told me many times, unlike those from the capital, who were focused only on their careers. She recounted stories about her friends and their brilliant grandchildren, some of whom had already entered primary school. When she talked about these things, she often wore a face clouded with disappointment.

For the most part, though, all through summer, our lives remained unremarkable except in one way. Once a week, the delivery man would come with a box of mushrooms. Some were fresh, others were dried. Not once were they the same variety, and we no longer tried to return them. In fact, we'd grown so accustomed to this routine that I'd started stocking our refrigerator with ingredients that paired well with mushrooms. Since we couldn't predict what type would be delivered next, I bought all kinds of meats and stored them in our freezer. I even got some butter after my mother-in-law told me that in recent years people in Yunnan had started to sear matsutake in butter. Once, to our surprise, we received a box of truffles, which we dipped in soy sauce and wasabi and ate like sashimi. We finished the whole bag in a day. I'd never heard of eating truffles in such abundance. But for the most part, my mother-in-law told me, wild mushrooms were prepared in traditional ways – stir-fried, grilled or added to soups.

I began looking forward to these deliveries. It was

only while cooking that my mother-in-law and I had some semblance of truly getting along. She gave the instructions and I did the work. The kitchen was a place where I fitted into her expectations. There, she must've felt she could convince herself that I was the daughter-in-law she'd hoped for. At first, I thought we were making progress. There were times I really believed that she was happy. But as we got on with our days, the other parts of my life closed in on her, denying her all her hopes and, in doing so, shaking me awake from my delusions too. She'd go on a walk every time I had a lesson. Things that had never bothered her before were now making her upset. Some days, she wouldn't even look at my piano.

Cooking mushrooms for Bowen became our only shared purpose – our happy escape. I purchased a mushroom encyclopedia and read up on all the ones we'd received. I was surprised by the fact that almost thirty per cent of all known species in the world are found in Yunnan because of the region's diverse terrain and mild climate.

One evening, Bowen came home and told us that his boss was sending him to Shanghai for two months. *It'll be a good opportunity for you two to bond*, he said, *since I won't be in the way*. His mother told him not to worry about us. I nodded along.

It just so happened that the day before Bowen's flight

was the day the deliveries stopped. We wanted to cook him a good meal before he left, so we'd been fully prepared for whatever mushrooms were to be brought to us that day. By three in the afternoon, the delivery man still hadn't come. We didn't have time to order any mushrooms online, so we went on a frantic journey across Beijing in search of Yunnan mushrooms. Supermarkets didn't carry any, leading us to try Yunnan restaurants. We were lucky and found someone willing to sell. The chef of a restaurant in Liangmaqiao was from Kunming and I watched as my mother-in-law chatted with him in their dialect. He explained that since it was towards the end of the wild mushroom season, they only had frozen ji zong mushrooms.

'That'll be fine,' my mother-in-law said. 'We can soak the mushrooms in their own oil, jar them and give them to Bowen to take with him. They'll keep for a few months this way.'

'I don't think he'll want to take the jar.'

'Song Yan, I don't want to criticise you, but you've got to be more attentive. Think about him a little more. It wouldn't hurt to take it with him, right?'

We took a taxi home. We were both exhausted and, on top of that, knowing Bowen would be gone for a while meant that neither of us had the motivation to speak to each other. I did, for a moment, consider breaking the silence, but all I could think about was the mushroom deliveries. If another box was to come the following week, without Bowen, I had no idea what we would do with the mushrooms. Bowen's appetite was more than ours combined. On the other hand, if we'd already received our last delivery, then what was next? Was this it? Did things really come and go so meaninglessly, leaving not a single trace of ever having been there?

At home, while I washed and tore the mushrooms into strips, my mother-in-law mixed together a bowl of aromatics: two types of Sichuan peppercorns, a big handful of dried red chilli peppers and half a head of garlic. In a wok, we heated some oil and deep-fried the mushrooms until they lost their moisture and shrivelled up, turning a golden colour. We added the aromatics and waited another thirty minutes before taking the wok off the heat. The mushrooms were now dark brown, glossy from the oil.

'How do we eat this?' I asked as I spooned the oil along with the mushrooms into empty pickle jars.

'There are so many things you can do,' my mother-in-law said. 'You can have it as a topping for congee, mix it in noodles, make fried rice or just have it by itself.'

'How does Bowen like to eat it?'

'Let's make noodles tonight. He can make the other stuff by himself, but he won't go to the trouble of making his own noodles.'

Bowen had always preferred rice to noodles. I'd

thought this was strange at first, since Yunnan is so famous for noodles. All he'd told me was that his taste for food didn't have to be defined by where he was from.

'Not everyone in Beijing likes to eat mutton hotpot,' he said. 'From what I remember, you don't like it, right?'

'Not particularly.'

'Well, there you go.'

For that reason, I'd never learned to make noodles very well, so my dough turned out too dry.

'Don't just add water like that!' my mother-in-law said when she saw me trying to save the dough by kneading it with wet hands. 'The moisture won't get to the inside of the dough ball. Get the steamer pot.'

She brought some water to a boil, turned off the heat and placed the dough on the steam tray for a few minutes.

'Just dust it with some flour if the surface gets too wet from the steam,' she explained. 'Next time, add more water to your dough.'

Bowen came home early that evening. He'd finished wrapping up and delegating all his work in Beijing. He said, somewhat proudly, that he was fully prepared to be on his way now.

'The mushroom deliveries didn't come today,' I said as we sat down for dinner. 'But Ma and I managed to buy some.'

'Go on,' my mother-in-law said. 'Eat as much as you

like. This might be the last meal of wild mushrooms you get this year.'

I spooned some mushroom oil onto Bowen's noodles.

'We jarred up some of this for you to take with you,' she said.

'It'll leak in my suitcase. Why don't you two keep it?'

I glanced at my mother-in-law, who was looking down at her bowl.

'Can you look out for a letter in the mail?' Bowen asked me. 'It should be from a dealership. Once it arrives, can you take pictures of the pages and send them to me? I don't know why they had to mail it to—'

'Is it so hard to listen to your mother for once?' my mother-in-law said rather loudly. She was still looking down.

Bowen stopped talking and put his chopsticks on his plate. He turned his chair towards his mother and sat at the end of his seat. He held her forearms in his hands.

'Ma, I'll do whatever you want. We both will.' He looked over at me and then immediately turned back. 'Now, I don't want to leave with you being upset. It'll worry me.'

Maybe we all become children to our children once we're old, I thought.

Bowen got up before sunrise. He packed a small suitcase with his work clothes and a single pair of jeans. I wrapped a jar of mushroom oil in layers of cling film and sealed it in a Ziploc bag.

'Isn't it weird that the mushroom deliveries stopped right before you're set to leave?' I said while he was putting his shoes on. 'It's like they came just for you.'

'Why don't you grow some yourself?'

'Grow what?'

'Mushrooms. Or anything you want.'

'But I don't know how,' I said.

'I'm sure you can learn.'

'I wouldn't dare to eat them, though.'

'It would give you something,' he said, standing up. 'You know, a little something to do. You don't have to eat them. Tell Ma that I'll call when I land, all right?'

'Sure thing.'

Before he got into the taxi, I gave him a strong hug that I hoped he would remember. I couldn't go back to sleep and went for a walk. It was a chilly morning, but I didn't bring a sweater. I bathed myself in the sensation of cold air blowing on my neck and arms. I enjoyed this. It reminded me that winter would soon arrive. I hadn't put my contact lenses in. Sometimes I would intentionally look around at the city this way, and images would become hazy and meld into one another. It was as if the madness of the streets had gone.

My mother-in-law was awake when I returned.

'Bowen left. You two didn't wake me,' she said, with a great deal of bitterness.

'It was early. He said he'll call when he lands.'

'Don't tell him to do that. He should be concentrating on his work.'

I couldn't figure out what she wanted me to do. I changed the topic.

'How about some breakfast?' I asked.

She shook her head. 'Message him and tell him not to worry about me and that there's no need to call,' she said.

She quickly gathered her embroidery tools and retreated into her room, as though she didn't want to spend an extra minute with me. I didn't blame her. It was stifling for the both of us to live under the same roof; we didn't really consider each other family. I knew I had blown it the night Bowen slept in the living room, keeping the luxury of our bed for myself. My mother-in-law must be doubting everything: my commitment to Bowen, my ability to be a good wife, her son's choice of a wife.

From then on, she rarely spoke to me, as if there was no point now that Bowen was gone. Similarly, I couldn't find the motivation to try and make amends. We stopped cooking together. At times, when we both happened to be in the living room, the silence between us would become oppressive to the point that I'd wish she would just yell at me. But when she did make the slightest movement or let out a hard sigh, I would panic and hide in the bedroom.

We might as well have been strangers – me getting on with my daily lessons, she with her embroidery. We ate separately most of the time, and when we didn't, we talked about trivial matters like groceries. Perhaps when you boiled it down, our relationship could be seen as intervals of shared eating and drinking, the basic human need to consume food and water. It reminded me of those documentaries I had watched of animals in deserts drinking at a waterhole.

One afternoon while my mother-in-law was taking a nap, I emptied the mailbox. It was crammed with brochures, mostly from real-estate firms. The letter that Bowen had told me to look out for was at the top of the stack. Towards the bottom, a small white envelope had slid between the flaps of a brochure. The words on it were written in neat handwriting. It was addressed to 'Ms Tian'.

Dear Ms Tian,

First of all, allow me to be clear, the 'Ms Tian' I am addressing this letter to is not a real person. At least, not as far as I know. But it does not matter the slightest to me – your name could be Julius Caesar for all I care. The reason I chose 'Tian' is nothing more than the fact that it was the first name that came to my mind, perhaps because my third-grade teacher was named Tian. But all of that is beside the point. This letter is addressed to whomever is reading it.

By this point in my letter, I hope you have realised that those mushrooms were sent to you by me. I have been receiving them from a stranger for some time but I no longer have a need for them. I hope they have brought you some enjoyment.

I try to be a forthright person, so I will tell you that I am writing because I would like you to come and visit me. I am a pianist. I was a pianist. Perhaps you know of me, I was once rather famous. But now I am afraid that I've lost everything, so I've decided to send you this letter out of desperation. I have a favour to ask – that's all I will tell you now. To communicate what the favour is in the form of a letter would not represent the immensity of what this would mean to me, if you were to accept.

My address is below. I look forward to welcoming you.

Yours truly,
Bai Yu

The address written on the letter was in the hutongs around Shichahai. I folded the letter and placed it inside the zipped pocket of my purse. As with everything I did nowadays, I found myself trying to hide it from my mother-in-law. This letter in particular – I knew I couldn't share it with anybody else. It felt private, intended, as if I had accidentally found it in the mouth of a stray dog yet it was somehow meant only for me. And now it belonged to me. I enjoyed the feeling.

Could this really be the same Bai Yu the world thought was dead? I searched his name online and found an article from ten years ago:

The famous piano prodigy Bai Yu has gone missing, two days before his European tour. According to his family, he has not left any messages, and the police department is not ruling out any possibilities. Bai Yu is best known for being the youngest pianist to win the Tchaikovsky International Music Competition. His perfectly executed, quiet yet rich performances of Claude Debussy's music have earned him recognition and praise from critics and audiences worldwide. This European tour would have been his first time performing in Cannes. The day before his disappearance, he expressed his excitement about being able to perform in the town where Debussy himself learned to play the piano.

For a few days, I mulled over the idea of paying a visit to Bai Yu. I wondered whether this could be a trap, but I couldn't figure out why someone would set a trap like this. What was there to gain from me? And why go through all the trouble of sending mushrooms? The more I thought about it, the less it made sense. But it was not until an incident during my lesson with little Shaobo that I set my mind on going to the address enclosed in the envelope.

That morning, I visited the food cart round the corner and brought home some buns for breakfast. When I came back, I found my mother-in-law crying in her bedroom. She had pierced her finger with a needle and she was sitting on the edge of the bed, looking down at the piece of fabric that was on her lap and the red-crowned crane that was embroidered on it. She had outlined parts of the wings with a silver thread that looked like mercury. The blood from her finger had stained the tail of the white crane. Under her breath, she was mumbling something over and over again. I couldn't make out what she was saying, but I could hear that it was either 'Bowen' or 'Boyan'.

I quickly grabbed some rubbing alcohol and a Band-Aid and sat down next to her, taking her hand to disinfect the wound. The finger had stopped bleeding already; all I needed to do was to clean up the blood and cover it.

'It's nothing serious,' I said, trying to calm her. 'Once I'm done here, let me bring you some of the buns that I got. And oh, that's a beautiful crane. The blood will come off easily if we wash it right away.'

After a long pause, she abruptly pulled her hand away from me and said, 'I want to go back to Yunnan. I want to go home.'

I considered how I would tell Bowen that his mother had packed her bags and left Beijing while he was away. He'd be sure I had mistreated her and I'd have no way of convincing him otherwise.

'But here is your home,' I said, and held her forearms in my hands, the way Bowen had done the night before he left. 'Let me know if there's something I can do better to make you feel at home here.'

'I'm imposing on your lives,' she mumbled.

'What nonsense! You're our mother.'

'It doesn't seem like you think of me as your mother,' she said. Her voice broke and her lips began to tremble, preventing her from saying more. She took a deep breath.

'I can't bear this any more,' she said. 'Watching you every day.'

'Let me know what it is that I've done and I will try my best to fix it.'

Though it was true that I hadn't been speaking to her much lately, I'd always been careful to be respectful to her. I made sure she was well taken care of, had nutritious meals three times a day, and brought her everything she needed. But now I knew what she wanted most was nothing like that. I waited for her to say it.

'The problem is that you haven't done anything,' she said, pulling away her arms. 'Anything a married woman should be doing.'

She looked straight ahead at the wall this whole time. I couldn't tell whether it was because it made her uneasy to criticise me or whether she simply didn't want to look at me any longer.

She continued. 'When will you stop focusing on these piano lessons and decide to raise a child? What's the point of Bowen working so hard if he doesn't have a family to come back to? I may not have been a good mother, but at least I gave life to two children. But look at you, Song Yan, what is the meaning of all these lessons?'

The mind is more brittle than many of us wish to believe. I felt a sudden urge to shout at her, to tell her that giving life was nothing to be celebrated if she could just as easily give away the very life she had created. I felt hot, as if I had eaten a torch. But things were already as bad as they could be and the last thing I wanted to tell Bowen was that an argument I'd had with his mother over having children had driven her away from Beijing.

So I gathered my things and left the apartment. Seeing that I still had a few hours before my afternoon lesson, I took a taxi to Nini's place. Nini is the person that for me most closely resembles what you would call a best friend. I've known her since childhood; we shared the same music theory teacher. She played the clarinet. Oftentimes she would visit me to practise duets together.

She grew up with her mother, who had died from lung cancer a few years ago. Unlike me, Nini had never aspired to become a professional musician. She worked as an assistant at a hair salon while still living in her mother's home. Her place was not so far from our new apartment, about a fifteen-minute drive, but in the taxi I became frustrated at the traffic; at the driver for not taking the emergency lane; at the pedestrians who crossed the roads too slowly. I didn't have a plan. I just knew I wanted to let words spill out of my mouth as they came, raw and unrestrained.

The lift was being repaired, so I had to walk up the stairs to the fifth floor. I was relieved to discover that Nini was home. When she opened the door, she smiled. It was a charming expression that I didn't want to spoil right away. I decided to wait and find a suitable moment to speak. She made me some instant coffee and picked at my hair.

'When was the last time you used conditioner?' she asked.

'I ran out a while ago.' I added some cold milk to the coffee and drank it all in one gulp.

I looked around. There were two empty instant-noodle cups on the kitchen counter, an overflowing rubbish bin, nail polish spilled under the TV cabinet and receipts lying everywhere, scrunched up into paper balls. After all these years of knowing her, I still couldn't believe that she could live like this.

There was a stack of photo albums on the coffee table. She grabbed a few of them and beckoned me over to sit down next to her.

'What luck that you came,' she said. 'I was just going through some old photos. I have a few with you in here.'

She began flipping through the albums and pointing at every person in the photos, telling me who they were. There were indeed a couple of photos of me back when I was still in primary school. In one of them, my father was sitting in front of the piano and I was on his lap. His hands were over mine. Nini was standing next to us with her clarinet. I wondered which piece we were playing. I half-heartedly scanned the smiling faces, remembering none of them, not even my own. A few times, I tried to tell her what I'd come here for, but my lips wouldn't move. I must have looked just like the people in those photos, frozen in a moment of silence.

Nini is not what you would call an intellectual person. She doesn't carry any ambitious dreams, but I haven't met anyone more content with their life than her. Even when her mother died, she was able to fully express how she felt, from denial to anger to crying for days on end, and finally to acceptance. That is not to say her wound has been healed. In fact, I could see her eyes moisten as she turned the pages in the albums. Unable to comprehend the sorrow of a lost mother, I imagined it to be profound and permanent, but Nini embraced it in a way that I knew I would never be able to. Perhaps it is her simple relationship with the world that attracted me to her at a young age. She has stripped the intricacies of human emotions down to their core, and she has accepted all of them, the bright as well as the dark.

After we looked at all the photos, we spent some time cleaning up the apartment. In the end, I left without having said anything important.

PIANO LESSONS

Little Shaobo was a fast learner. By this time, he had already mastered a few basic melodies. His hands, though small, were agile, and I felt fulfilment in watching him improve. His father seemed proud as well, the way fathers do, the way my father was once proud of me. I have clear memories of the day I passed my Grade 1 exam – the weight of my father's large hands resting on my shoulders, squeezing them. I admired how those hands were able to play the most wonderful sounds.

My father never gave me lessons. He didn't have the time. We had two pianos at home: a grand and an upright. It never made much sense to me why we had two. Our place wasn't so big that we could both play at the same time and not hear the other person. On the occasions when I used the grand piano, I would always make sure to adjust the seat to my father's liking after I finished my session. Once, he thanked me for it. My father and I would often sit next to the stereo and listen to music together. He would show me photos of all the

great concert halls in the world, mainly the ones he
hadn't performed at: Carnegie Hall, the Musikverein,
Boston Symphony Hall. He explained the history, the
architecture and the acoustics to me. Tokyo Opera City
Concert Hall was his favourite. He would tell me that
one day I'd become a better pianist than him and
play on these stages. He couldn't have guessed just how
different the future was to be from the one he'd prom-
ised me.

Little Shaobo was practising arpeggios when he
asked me, 'Ms Song, can I hear you play something?
With both hands.'

'Let me see,' I said. 'What would you like me to play?'

'The hardest piece you know!'

I thought about his request. I had never considered
which was the hardest piece I knew. Of course, there
were pieces that were technically more challenging
than others, but that wasn't what little Shaobo had
asked; he didn't say, 'Play the most technically difficult
piece you know,' he used the word 'hardest'. There was
no way, in that moment, I could think of what that
might be and perform it for little Shaobo. I panicked,
and wanting to get it over with quickly, I picked a
Chopin étude that I still had memorised by heart and
hoped that little Shaobo would be impressed. He
watched my hands keenly while his father stood at the
doorway and listened. When I finished, they both
clapped.

After I left the lesson, an unbearable sense of guilt wrapped around me and tightened like vacuum packaging. I hadn't given my student a sincere, deliberate answer. Out of my old fear of disappointing someone, I had come up with something rushed and dishonest. What bothered me more was that if time were to rewind, I would do the same thing again. I had even failed as a teacher; what else was I good for?

I walked into an empty restaurant and ordered some baijiu. It had been a while since I'd drunk alcohol, and the burning sensation felt painfully yet reassuringly familiar.

I was rather drunk when I fished out the letter from my bag, paid the bill and staggered to Qian Gan Hutong. I'm not sure how long it took me to get there, but the sky was dark by the time I arrived. It was challenging to navigate the old hutongs, and it wasn't until quite late that I managed to locate the address written on the letter.

The vermilion-painted wooden gate to the property was slightly open, but I banged the copper handle against it anyway. There was no response. I knocked again. Once more, I was met with silence. Reasoning that since I had gone to all the trouble of getting here, and not knowing what else to do, I leaned my weight against the gate and stumbled in. Finding my balance, I tiptoed around a screen wall, through another gate and finally into the open courtyard. It was shaped like a square, enclosed by three single-storey buildings and the wall behind me. Though I'd spent my whole life in Beijing, I'd never been inside one of these courtyards before. Like the Forbidden City, the door and windows of the main building faced south, into the courtyard. This way, the head of the household could bathe in the luxury of cooler summers and warmer winters. I imagined the layout of the courtyard to be similar to the other homes in this neighbourhood. The windows were dark. The moon shone on a large, dusty pot with nothing growing in it. The place looked desolate. There weren't even any trees.

'Good evening!' I yelled.

In the shadows, a red bicycle was leaning against the wall. I walked closer and ran my fingers along the frame. It was dusty and rusted. I tried to move it, but it made a loud creaking sound.

I was about to shout something again when I heard the door to the main house crack open. I couldn't see clearly, but a man was there. I walked over to take a better look at his face.

'Please don't be so loud,' he said. 'I don't want complaints from the neighbours.'

Up close, Bai Yu looked the same as he had when my father took me to see him perform. It was the only time I saw him live. He'd played a Prokofiev concerto with the Chicago Symphony Orchestra on their China tour. We sat in the front, at the very left side of the stage, so

all I could see was Bai Yu's back. The only moment I
had a clear view of his face was when he walked out and
towards the conductor. He'd seemed like a man whose
age, past a certain point, would be impossible to tell
from his appearance. His hair was partially grey, and he
could have been twenty-five or fifty, there was no way
to be sure.

'You're really Bai Yu, aren't you?' I said. 'Have you
been here this whole time?'

He was in a black suit. I thought about how pleased
my father would be to find out that Bai Yu was still alive.

'Do come in first. I don't want to be rude,' he said,
turning around and guiding me into his home.

I hesitated, but my curiosity prevailed and I followed
him.

'Allow me to brew you some tea,' he said, as he
turned on the lights and went into another room.

I sat on a redwood chair and waited for him. The
walls had cracks all across them. There wasn't much
furniture – only a small table and two chairs in the main
room. The heater must have been turned off; the air was
bitingly cold. I wondered how he could've stayed unnoticed for so long here, dead in the centre of Beijing.

He returned with a pot of tea and sat on the other
chair. He walked gracefully, just as he'd moved on stage
that day when he strode out slowly, shook the conductor's hand, gave a barely noticeable bow and lowered
himself onto the piano bench. He'd taken his time to

adjust the height of the seat. During the years he was active, there were some people who criticised him for often intentionally provoking the audience by taking too long, but most had viewed his meticulousness as essential to his performance.

He sat down in front of me in the same manner. He couldn't adjust the height of the chair, of course, but his posture was perfect. He poured the tea carefully and placed it on the table.

'I imagine you're rather cold, Julius Caesar,' he said.

'My name is not Julius Caesar.'

'Like I said in my letter, it does not matter to me what your name is.'

Under normal circumstances, these words would've been rude, but I didn't sense any ill intentions from him.

'My name is Song Yan,' I said. 'Even if you don't care.'

'Have you been consuming alcohol?'

'A bit.'

'Well, that also doesn't matter to me. As long as you can remember what I am about to say.'

'You haven't answered my question,' I said. 'Have you been living here all these years?'

'Forgive me. I cannot answer your question.'

'Are you a ghost?'

'Human, ghost or god, what difference does it make if you can hardly remember what you were in the first place?'

'Then what is it that you want to be?'

'That is precisely why I had you come here. Please, come with me.'

He stood up again and walked towards the room to the left. I followed him. There was a Steinway & Sons in the centre of the room, a bench in front of it, and nothing more.

I looked at Bai Yu and found him staring at the piano, but as I observed him more carefully, he was not so much staring at the piano as he was staring at the air hovering around the piano. His expression reminded me of my mother-in-law's face when she talked about Boyan.

'Do you play?' he asked.

I nodded, rather dramatically. My head felt incredibly heavy.

'I'm a piano teacher,' I said.

'That will save us a lot of time.' He lifted the cover of the bench, grabbed some pieces of paper from the top of a rather large pile, sifted through them and handed them to me.

'Here. This will do. Play this,' he said. 'It shouldn't be too difficult.'

I looked at the papers. They were the sheet music for Debussy's *Rêverie*, one of the composer's early works. It was a piece that I'd played as a teenager.

I opened the lid of the piano while Bai Yu stood, wearing the same expression. When I sat down, I thought about changing the height of the bench but decided against it. I flattened out the sheet music and placed it on the rack.

Though it had been a while since I'd played the piece, like Bai Yu said, it wasn't a difficult one. Under the yellow light, I began playing. The last time I'd performed on a Steinway was when I was still at university. The keys on this one were stiffer, more demanding. I'd been accustomed to playing Yamahas, so when the sounds came out with so much colour and subtlety, I had trouble adjusting. I tried to balance the soft and fluid tone of the piece with a sense of firmness at the tips of my fingers. I imagined a river at night, serene and contained under the lights in the city and then flowing into a forest, becoming dark and mysterious, winding through unexplored terrains. When I finished, I looked over at Bai Yu. He had not moved.

I've always been struck that silence in a room comes not immediately the music is over, but a few moments after the last note has finished reverberating. When the sounds of the night returned, Bai Yu was the first to speak.

'Thank you for that. But I'm afraid it wasn't good enough.'

I was upset.

'Certainly you can't expect me to play like you,' I said and stood up from the seat. A page of the sheet music blew off the stand.

'I don't want you to play like me. The truth is, I can't play any more.'

He walked over and, with much care, picked up the sheet music and arranged the pages back together, in order.

'The more time I spent with the piano,' he continued, 'the more it seemed like my hands didn't belong to me. The sounds didn't come from me. I became frightened to the point that every time I was sitting at the piano, I couldn't help but feel there wasn't a "me" at all. So I stopped playing.'

I thought for a moment. 'And now you want me to play for you?' I asked. 'What if you'd gone to all this trouble and found someone who didn't even know how to play the piano?'

'But you do know,' he said, as though it was the obvious answer.

'How did you find my address then?'

'By pure chance, I suppose.'

It wasn't easy to believe, but he sounded as if he was telling the truth.

'What do you think the sound of being alive is?' he said.

'What?'

He paused briefly, as if to finalise the decision in his head, and then he said, 'I want you to help me find the sound of being alive.'

We both looked down at the sheet music in his hands.

'The sound is there,' he said. 'In the piano. I know that. It is loud and strong. I've heard it before.'

His hands were so thin – they were the colour of raw cashews, and I imagined that they were cold. I couldn't think of a way to help him. If he had asked for anything else, I would've done my best to give him the answer he needed. I would've done it for my father, for me, for Bai Yu himself, simply for the reason that I wanted to help him. But I had no idea how I could do something with the piano that even Bai Yu couldn't achieve. He was the perfect pianist.

I turned round to leave. He didn't say anything to stop me. In the courtyard, I looked into the house again. It seemed that, within the blink of an eye, those sheets of paper in his hands could transform into ashes, as could he, and together they might be blown away and vanish from this world.

* * *

I spent the following days listening to Bai Yu's old recordings and contemplating his words. *I couldn't help but feel there wasn't a 'me' at all.* I tried to decipher what he'd meant by that, but no matter how intently I listened, I couldn't figure out what it was. His technique was flawless and his music had a signature eeriness and poise that allowed his audiences to recognise that he was behind it. As I listened to the tracks repeatedly, what struck me most were the deep silences that could be heard in his music. Like the soundless moments before an earthquake. It was as if this silence was more resonant than the mere absence of sound.

During those days, I often heard my mother-in-law sobbing at night. I spent as little time as possible at home and went to my students' apartments for all of my lessons, coming up with the excuse that our building was undergoing renovations that would make it too loud for piano lessons. When I taught Yuyu, I found myself listening to her the same way I studied Bai Yu's recordings. I tried to identify something that I couldn't even describe myself; an abstract thing that I wasn't quite sure existed. *The sound of being alive*, as Bai Yu put it. After Yuyu passed her exam, she'd told me that she wanted to take a break before starting the Grade 8 pieces, so I decided to assign *Rêverie* to her.

I resisted demanding that she adhere strictly to the directions on the sheet music (which I had always done before) and encouraged her to insert herself into the music.

'Think of *Rêverie* as a story that can be told from different points of view and try to tell it from yours,' was the best advice I could come up with.

I was relieved when she didn't ask me to elaborate on what I meant. To be entirely honest, I didn't really know myself. She gave it some thought, frowned in confusion, and nodded hesitantly.

To avoid going home, I'd picked up the habit of having a few drinks after my lessons. It helped me fall asleep, eased the anxiety I had developed around my mother-in-law and was overall quite enjoyable. It had quickly developed into an almost sacred routine. I didn't enjoy being at bars – I dreaded the thought of becoming a regular somewhere – so I would buy a few bottles of beer and go to Chaoyang Park. Parks were my favourite places, especially the ones in the busiest districts. There was a generosity that could be felt there. Amidst buildings that were increasingly close to the sky, space in parks extended outwards. From time to time, I'd read in magazines about wealthy people living in penthouses, the higher up the better. All the developers seemed to be outdoing each other to design the tallest skyscraper, like the newest one in Guomao that seems to rise all the way into the clouds. To me, there is something to be said about being close to the ground. If I could, I'd always choose to live with my feet touching the earth. I sleep better that way.

Autumn's gold had been waning into a dusty colour. Every night felt colder than the last. I was at the park late one afternoon, three beers in and listening in on a young man's conversation with his father.

'Don't you like the trees, Father?' the son said. 'Some of them are so splendid. They must've been here for decades.'

I couldn't help but chuckle at the formality of the

word 'Father'. The younger man had such a solemn expression and his chest was held so high that he looked as if he was in a stage play. I kept listening.

'Back home,' the old man said, 'we've finally managed to cut down all the trees to make way for roads. Those trees were much older than these little ones.'

'I haven't been back in so many years, I hardly remember what the village looks like,' the son said. 'That's quite sad, don't you think? And now all the trees are gone.'

The old man clutched his hands together behind his back and kept walking. 'Never thought about that,' he said.

My phone rang.

'I'm going to Munich,' Bowen said.

'You're what?' My mind was still on the trees that had been cut down to make space for cars.

'Just for a week. I'm at the airport now.'

'Oh. Would you like Ma to know?'

'Where are you? It sounds windy.'

'I'm at the park. Should I tell Ma?'

'Don't bother. It'll be better for her to think I'm still in Shanghai. She'll be less worried. How is she doing?'

'Well, she misses you, I think. But she's healthy.' I paused for a second and then added, 'We both miss you.'

I wanted to say, *you're the only thing keeping us together*, but instead I smiled into the phone, hoping he'd hear it somehow. It was true. I missed Bowen. I missed his leather shoes by the door, his legs hoisted on the coffee table, his trimmed nails flicking a cigarette. I'd never found any of these things particularly charming before – in fact, he'd often be so focused on his reading that he would miss the ashtray, and I'd have to wipe the ashes from the floor – but I valued the familiarity of it all, as if it was a sign that I had successfully incorporated his life into my own.

'I'll be back home in a few weeks,' Bowen said. 'Take good care of Ma. She's lived a hard life and she's getting old now. I'm counting on you.'

'I understand.' Through the phone, I could hear a woman announcing something related to a flight to Jakarta. It wasn't Bowen's flight.

'So what's for dinner?' he asked.

'Maybe ji zong mushrooms!' I joked. The deliveries had stopped long ago, and without him here neither of us would go to the trouble of looking for ji zong mushrooms.

'Well, I'll text you when I land.' He didn't laugh.

'Sure.'

What an irrational thing – I felt as if he was leaving home all over again, even though he'd been away this whole time. The result of all these weeks was that I had grown accustomed to him being in Shanghai, and I had fused that little fact into my daily life. I suppose missing someone isn't so much the consequence of

distance – it comes from the disruption of the sense-
less routines that have been formed in the mind.
Shanghai or Munich. What did it matter? The fact was,
he wasn't here.

The sun had moved on by now, reminding me to go
home. I finished the rest of the beer and walked towards
the exit of the park. The son and his old man were out
of sight. I wondered whether Bowen was referring to
Boyan when he said his mother had lived a difficult life.
Perhaps he knew that his mother had told me about
her, or maybe he was considering telling me himself.

The wind picked up all of a sudden. Dead leaves were
blown left and right. When I walked up to the bus stop,
a couple were already waiting there. The man was thin
and wore rimless glasses, the woman was in a rose-
coloured turtleneck and a milky white coat. Her hair
hung right above her shoulders, grazing them only
when she turned her head to talk to the man. She had
her back to me. As I watched her hair, I was suddenly
aware of something important. This person in front of
me, or any person, for that matter, could be Boyan.

I entertained that thought for a while. I observed her
closely and noticed that her shoulders were actually
rather similar to Bowen's – slim and sloping. I followed
them onto a bus. It wasn't the one I had planned to take,
but it would take me to Hujialou. From there I could
walk home.

The bus was packed and I stood behind the woman.

I still couldn't see her face. She took off one of her knitted gloves and held it out to the man.

'Smell this,' she said. 'Does it smell like me?'

Her hoarse voice cracked at the second 'smell'. She must've caught a cold recently. The man lowered his nose to the glove and his glasses almost fell off his face, so he hurriedly straightened his posture and pushed them back up.

'It does a little,' he said, blushing.

Wang Xiao and Ruya came for dinner that night. They arrived with a bag of takeout from a Chaoshan restaurant that I liked. They also brought along a few bottles of Red Star erguotou.

'We thought you must be lonely!' Ruya said while lifting the bottles up in the air. Her voice filled the entire apartment.

Wang Xiao nudged her arm. 'Bowen's mother is here.'

'Oh, right,' she whispered.

She turned to me and asked, 'Where is she? Does she want to eat with us? Have a drink, maybe?'

I knocked on my mother-in-law's door and asked whether she was hungry. I waited a few seconds. When I understood that she wasn't going to respond, I told the couple that she must've had dinner already and gone to bed by now.

'She sleeps early,' I lied. 'Right after it turns dark.'

They seemed to believe me and we sat down around the table. Wang Xiao opened one of the Red Stars.

'This will warm us up,' he said as he poured.

We ate and drank and conversed about things that I would forget the day after. I got rather drunk, so I offered to play the piano for them.

'Wouldn't that wake up your mother-in-law?' Wang Xiao said.

'Don't you worry about that!' I slapped him on the shoulder. 'She doesn't care.'

'Let her play!' Ruya said. Her elbow was resting on the table, and her chin was cupped in her hand.

'Let me play!' I echoed as I opened the lid of the piano. 'What should I play?'

'Oh, I *love* Chopin,' Ruya said. The word 'love' came out breathily.

'Are you sure?' Wang Xiao said. By this point, his voice was about as loud as the piano. Even when he's had a few drinks too many, he's still a polite man.

I sat down. After a moment, the couple fell silent too, and they stared at me while I stared at the keys. I began to play *Rêverie*. I no longer had the piece memorised by heart, but I didn't stop until the end. I kept playing, one wrong note after another. It wasn't music and it wasn't beautiful. A fortress in me had been breached and sounds escaped from it only to become trapped within the walls of the apartment.

I don't remember much of what I played that night,

but I can say with certainty that I got the final chord right. When I first learned to memorise *Rêverie*, I often played that chord too early. It seemed a simple mistake to fix, but my brain refused to cooperate. Soon enough, my piano teacher grew frustrated with me. When I finally got it right, she was so spent that we immediately moved on to another piece and she never asked me to play *Rêverie* again.

'I think Song Yan's had a little too much to drink,' Ruya said when I finished. She brought my glass to me and said, 'I also think she should have another.'

Wang Xiao pulled her away and seized the glass from her. He told her that it was already past midnight and asked her whether she would be OK with saying good-night. She looked over at me. I pretended to yawn, and upon seeing that, she agreed to leave.

After I sent them out the door, my mother-in-law hobbled out of her room. On her way to the kitchen, she pulled out a handkerchief from her pocket and pressed it over her nose.

'I'm sorry about the smell,' I said. 'Wang Xiao came by with some liquor.'

She walked past me into the kitchen and after a few minutes, re-emerged with a glass of hot water.

'Song Yan, this is Bowen's home. Your home,' she said in a soft, sighing voice. 'It will never be my home. I'm old now. I don't want to feel like a guest for the rest of my life.'

It was as if she knew that I wasn't going to respond
this time and that I wasn't going to ask her to stay any
more. Before closing her bedroom door, she said, 'I'll
talk to Bowen when he's back.'

I wish I could've told her that we will feel constrained
anywhere, but freedom can still be found in those same
places. But back then I didn't know that. I had resigned
myself to the belief that she would never feel at home
with us, no matter how much we provided for her.

Maybe it was the alcohol, but for the first time in a
long while, I slept soundly that night.

SWALLOWS

The twentieth of November was a clear and still day. It had been exactly four years since Nini's mother died. I've spent this day with Nini every year since then. It feels appropriate to the both of us – I am the only one of her friends who knew her mother well. Nini doesn't have a car, so I'd pick her up and we'd make stops to buy joss paper, pastries and a bottle of her mother's favourite red wine before driving west, out of the city, towards the cemetery.

Nini didn't talk much on the way there. Once we merged onto the highway, she made sure the wine was secure on her lap and closed her eyes. I couldn't imagine she was asleep, but I knew not to speak to her. That worked for me; I never enjoyed chatting much while I was driving. I put on some music and focused on the road. Earlier that day, I had found an old CD that my father burned and gave to me when I started university. It's a collection of his favourite performances, from Rachmaninoff's Piano Concerto No. 2 played by Gary

Graffman and the New York Philharmonic Orchestra, to his first teacher's interpretation of Liszt's 'Liebestraum' No. 3 in A-flat major, to a few Debussy pieces from Bai Yu's solo recital in Shanghai, and lastly, to my first performance. Mine's the final track; it is the only piece my father has ever composed himself. He named it after me – *Swallows*.

I've heard my father play the piece many times. It's a simple composition, but when you listen to it more intently, you'll find a hidden depth. Like looking into a cave and seeing something sparkling at you. Could it be a gem? Or a golden tooth? The music paces at the entrance but never takes you inside. That's the kind of piece it is.

Somewhere towards the second half of the piece, I realised I had forgotten I was the one playing. No matter how I tried, I couldn't picture myself pressing on those keys and producing those sounds. The music came to me as undeniably as the feeling of still air touching skin, as if no one was playing it and it had just always been there.

A feeling of horror surged into my head and my vision went blank. I clasped the wheel and tried to recall whether the highway ahead was straight. The melody of *Swallows* continued to flow into my ears. Was it really me, playing those notes? I scanned my memory of our apartment that day – Yamaha piano, walnut floors, Nini and her mother in the audience. We were having one of those New Year's Day concerts that my father religiously hosted every year. He had a friend visiting from Italy who'd brought us a few boxes of cantucci biscuits, which all night I'd been too nervous to eat since I was the last to perform. The friend was a classical violinist who played for an Italian orchestra – impressive, at the time, for a Chinese musician. He'd entered the door with the biscuits in one hand and his violin in the other. I could see him sitting on our sofa with his instrument on his lap. I remembered most of what had happened up until the moment I sat down at the piano to play. Then there was nothing but a white fog.

It didn't take too long before I could see again. I looked over at Nini. Her eyes were still closed and she didn't seem to have noticed anything. My loss of vision must've lasted only a few seconds. I turned off the CD player. For a while, the music lingered, gently humming in my head until bit by bit it melted away into the silent car.

Nini sat on the ground in front of her mother's headstone and opened the wine bottle.

'Dang. Forgot to bring a glass,' she said. 'Good thing that you always drank straight from the bottle.'

She took a sip and then held it up in the air.

'Cheers,' she said. Then, ceremonially, in a horizontal motion, she poured half of the wine into the soil before corking the bottle and placing it on the ground next to all the food we'd brought.

The rest of our visit went as usual. We cleaned the grave, burned the joss paper, talked to her mother, talked to each other. After all that and before we left, I held Nini's hand while she cried and choked and screamed at the sky.

On the way back, Nini was much more cheerful, as if a huge weight had been taken off her mind. I didn't turn on the music.

'Can you drop me off at the salon?' she said.

'How's work been?'

'Still not making much money.' She smiled. 'But I like it. Little money means little work, so I can go home and relax.'

Occasionally, I found myself envious of the life she'd chosen, as well as of her will to choose it in the first place. At those times I would feel hopeless, as I knew that even if I was given the chance to live like her, I couldn't feel happy.

'Well,' I said. 'Would you consider playing the clarinet again? Why don't you bring it over sometime and let's play together.'

'You know I don't remember how to play like I used to.'

I'm the same, I thought of saying. Bai Yu's voice was like a drumstick tapping on the back of my head. *There wasn't a 'me' at all*, he was repeating. Perhaps now I understood him a little better. We pour a bit of ourselves into everything we do, every note we play, I thought, and unwittingly, one fragment at a time, we leave ourselves in the past.

After I dropped Nini off, I drove to Bai Yu's place. It felt like something I had to do. The front gate was still unlocked, so I just walked in. During the day, the courtyard looked much older. No one had swept the leaves from the ground. There was a stray black cat with a white tail sitting on the seat of the red bicycle. It ran away when I approached. I knocked on the door and waited patiently. After a few minutes, Bai Yu came out.

'You're back,' he said.

Time seemed to have flowed differently here. He looked exactly the same as when I had left him the other night, his hair brushed to the same side, parted at the same spot. There was one strand that hung over his left eye.

'I'm here to play for you again,' I said.

He looked at me with the indifference of an owl. I stared back at him.

'Come in,' he said.

I walked straight towards the piano room. The lid was open, so I sat down. I didn't look at him, but I knew he was right where he stood last time, waiting. I began to play *Swallows*, praying I'd be able to remember the day of the recording. To my surprise, the moment I pushed down the first key, the rest came effortlessly. I could hear exactly what it sounded like. The cave. The thing that was sparkling inside, just out of reach.

At some point, Bai Yu walked up to me. He was standing behind me when I finished. I tried to turn, but he put his hands over my shoulders and held them in place.

'Play that again,' he said. Then, without rushing, he lowered his hands over mine, barely touching them. His face was next to my ear. He smelled like melting wax, which I thought was exactly how the house smelled. It was as though he had become part of it.

'Play that again,' he repeated.

The whole time, he kept his hands there. They moved with me as if they knew the piece too. Even though he wasn't touching the keys, it felt as if he was the one playing and I was quite literally standing in the way between him and the piano.

And then there it was. I heard it again. The bottomless hole I had always feared when listening to his performances. As we played, my father's mysterious cave was becoming deeper and heavier. If we kept going, maybe I'd at last discover what was lying in those places I could never see before.

But my hands froze. I knew this feeling. It was like those instincts I'd had as a child that were more potent and accurate than anything the adult mind could reason. I felt fear in my gut. I was afraid that if we continued, I would discover that in those places there was nothing at all.

Bai Yu slowly withdrew his arms and straightened his back. He took a deep breath and held it there, as if trying to fill a void inside him. Finally, I admitted to myself that I had come back here not because of curiosity, or music, or some noble act of kindness. I had been drawn to him because I had a void in me too.

'Can I come back?' I asked.

'I'll be waiting.'

JULIA

Ruya called me in the middle of the night, troubled and confused. She said that Julia had obtained her number and had been phoning her multiple times these past days, repeating the same thing.

'I must talk to her,' Julia would say.

Ruya told me that when she got back from her trip to Yunnan, she hadn't been prepared to be tracked down by Bowen's ex-wife. I wanted to explain to her that she couldn't expect to insert herself into other people's lives without becoming entangled in them. But at the end of the day, this was our affair and I didn't want any of it to cause problems for her, so I told her to give Julia my number.

'Thank you, thank you,' she kept repeating. All the tautness in her voice had vanished. 'Let me know how it goes. I'm so relieved. I can finally sleep well now.'

But now I couldn't sleep. It was almost two in the morning. I crept into the living room, opened a bottle of beer and sat by the window with a novel. Very soon

I realised that I couldn't focus on reading at all. What could Julia possibly want? What should I say to her? I tried to rehearse for the phone call, but since I couldn't predict what Julia was going to say, any preparations were going to be pointless.

I knew Bowen was on his flight back to Shanghai. Maybe he was flying over me right now. I saw a light come on in the building across the road, the same one I'd seen months ago, when my mother-in-law was telling me about the red soil that enveloped the land she called home.

Out there nothing had changed. Inside, things had stirred.

The next morning, looking for something to distract myself with, I remembered Bowen's suggestion and decided to research how to grow mushrooms at home. It only took a few minutes to find that they sold mushroom kits on Taobao. According to the vendor's instructions, all I had to do was keep the bag moist and out of sunlight and soon enough all kinds of fungi would grow. Oyster, poplar, wood ear, enoki . . . The list was long.

I read the reviews. Most of them were by mothers buying the kits for their children's entertainment, once toys weren't fun enough any more. One woman wrote that she wanted her son to know how his food was grown and where it came from. I found it shocking that many of the reviewers cooked and ate the mushrooms they grew. I couldn't figure out whether they were fearless or ignorant. What if the seller had the wrong seeds and the mushrooms were poisonous?

I browsed through the options. Towards the bottom of the list, I saw ji zong mushrooms. According to the information on the page, they were more complicated to grow and they wouldn't be the same kind as those that grow in the wild. I couldn't just keep them in the bags. They required soil. I decided to start with something easier, so I selected a few that seemed straightforward and added them to my shopping cart.

Checking out, I saw a few books I had saved before Bowen left. *Perfect Pregnancy*. *Successful Pregnancy: Nutritious Recipes*. I selected everything and paid. The packages would be here the next week.

Julia's call came the following evening while I was on a walk.

'There's something I must tell Bowen,' she said.

She had a strong accent, similar to that of my mother-in-law. Her tone had a flatness to it, as if she had disguised her real voice with something fake.

'He vanished from my life,' she went on, after I didn't say anything. 'Moved on.'

She sounded accusatory, as if I was the one who'd left her.

I sat down on the kerb. 'Are you telling me that you want him back?' I asked.

Her voice abruptly broke into a series of disconcerting squeals. After she stopped laughing, she took a deep breath and continued.

'I think I'd rather find out he's dead.'

She coughed a few times.

'Song Yan, right?' she said. 'What a graceful name. Can you tell Bowen that our town turned orange?'

'What?'

'It started with orange dust in the air. We thought it was pollen at first, but it's almost winter now and it's only getting worse. It's already covered the surface of the entire river that runs through our town. I can send you a picture if you like.'

'I'm going to hang up if you keep talking nonsense.'

'Tell him that our child drowned in the river.'

She phrased this as if it was the most ordinary fact in the world. Perhaps it was the only way she could articulate it; hear it come out of her own mouth. Now, I remember the sound of words being forced out with each breath of hers, and the last few coming out more like a whisper, as if the softer she said it, the less true it was. But at the time, try as I might, my mind wouldn't focus on the tragedy of a dead child and instead clung tightly to the words *our child*, knowing exactly what she'd meant, and that what she was saying might be true. Immediately, I felt pain, physical pain, as if I had fallen from a tower and the impact had pierced every part of my body: my skin, my bones, my lungs. It coursed through my veins. I knew I was breathing, but I couldn't feel it. I could see my breath in the cold air, which was worse, because if I wasn't breathing, I could just force myself to do it. Now I couldn't do anything. My lungs were working fine, but I was suffocating.

She waited while I struggled to find something to say. Her breathing coming through the phone became much louder to me.

'Does he know,' I eventually managed to say, 'that he had a child?'

'I guess he decided not to tell you,' she said. 'When we found out I was pregnant, he told me that he didn't want to keep the baby. We argued every day until one night he bought a ticket to Beijing and never came back. He sent the divorce papers through a lawyer and left me stranded like a dead tree in a desert. We haven't spoken since then.'

I could've told myself that this had to be a lie and none of it made any rational sense, but I couldn't hang up the phone. The masked voice she had begun with started to make way for the real one beneath, like clouds clearing up over a mountain.

'Our child was a boy, and he was eight years old,' she continued. 'You know what? Sometimes I think that maybe he was never supposed to live. If I had just killed him back then, at least Bowen would still be here with me now and life would be manageable somehow.'

She paused. There it was again. *Our child.* I heard her move the phone to her other ear.

'The dust has covered all the trees along the riverbank,' she continued when she understood that I wasn't going to say anything. 'It seems like with every passing day there is more in the air.'

She stopped talking, more deliberately this time. I didn't have to ask her why she couldn't tell Bowen directly. Maybe, like she said herself, Bowen had left her to be a lone tree, and now she wanted to burn and destroy everything around him, including me. Or maybe she thought I was the only person who could understand her, however imperfectly. Or maybe – and more likely – the reasons were too complex to be spoken and what mattered was not what they were but the fact that she knew, and I knew too, that I was the one who had to hear this.

I told her I'd tell him. I needed some time alone to think.

'It happened the night the dust landed on the river,' she said. 'He was playing by the riverbank. The water must've looked like land to him. He fell in and nobody was there to help.'

She sounded as if she had more to say, but her voice broke, and then, rather abruptly, she told me goodbye, talk soon, as if we were old acquaintances who had run into each other in a lift.

I found a quiet street and tried to steady my heartbeat. I took deep breaths, forced myself to focus, closed
my eyes and tried to make an account of everything I'd
heard. But none of it worked. I called Bowen. He
wouldn't answer his phone. Perhaps he was asleep or
still at work. I dialled his number seven or eight times
until he picked up. There was loud music in the background, a few voices singing into microphones, and
others yelling and laughing over the music. No matter
how many times I repeated Bowen's name, he didn't
come to the phone. Not even when I told him that Julia
had called me. I asked him where he was, who he was
with, whether he knew that he had a child and that the
child was now gone forever. I asked him if he cared. I
shouted at him, on and on. Each word was met with
those same chaotic happy sounds feeding over from
the other end. A woman walked by and, upon seeing
me, sped up her footsteps and rushed away. I told
Bowen about the orange dust in the air, about his boy
who was given the chance to live but never had the
opportunity to grow up, about Julia, about his mother
and how she seemed to despise me, about how that
woman at the bus station could have been Boyan. I told
him how unfortunate I thought it was that he had
become just as much a stranger to his family as I was.
When I finished, I hung up.

I clenched my hair and cried. I slapped myself across
the face. It stung and made me cry even harder. I knew

that he had accidentally picked up the call. The only reason I could finally scream at him was because he wasn't listening.

I stuffed the phone back into my pocket. Then, like a squirrel returning to its den at night, I hailed a taxi to Bai Yu's house.

*   *   *

The mushroom kits and pregnancy books I'd bought arrived on the same day. I threw away the books and opened up the kits. Each one was wrapped in plastic and consisted of cylindrical shapes made up of what the manual referred to as mushroom substrate. It went on to explain that the white, granite-like coating on the surface was mycelium. None of these words meant anything to me as I had no clue how mushrooms were grown. Maybe my mother should have bought these for me when I was young, but I'm certain that she'd never have thought of something like that.

My childhood was rather uneventful. Aside from school, most of it was spent practising piano. I must've gone on a few trips with my parents, but I could hardly recall any of them. Whenever I think back, I see my father sitting at the piano playing the sweetest sounds; my mother standing next to the calamondin orange tree, listening. But as I think further, I can't point to a single moment that was actually as flawlessly peaceful as this. And so it seems that the most vivid memory I have of growing up can't be considered a real memory at all. But that is the charm of childhood, isn't it? We remember it as being either filled with bliss or filled with pain, and as we grow up, we begin living every day in between.

A week had passed since Julia phoned me and I hadn't managed to mention a word to Bowen, not when he was listening, anyway. In fact, I had been avoiding him entirely. He'd called me back once, but I chose not to pick up. After a few rings, while I was still staring at his name on the screen, he hung up, the name changed into a missed-call notification and he hadn't tried again since.

Looking around, everything that belonged to Bowen, including the apartment itself, seemed to be either closing in on me or drifting away. Oftentimes it felt like things were going both nearer and further at once, as if the closer they were, the less I could believe that they ever existed.

I went to see Bai Yu every day. I would play for him and his hands would hover over mine. Even though they seldom touched, sometimes I could feel his hands better than my own. I liked watching the reflection of our hands in the surface of the polished black instrument – how they moved together, stopped together; how everything else faded into the background and only our hands were visible; how close they were; and how alive they seemed.

We played all kinds of pieces, including ones I'd never learned before. He wouldn't speak much, and I chose not to ask him whether he had found the sound he was looking for yet. I didn't want to hear the answer. It felt as though once I asked, he'd be gone again.

I unfolded the instructions sheet that came with one of the mushroom kits.

Grow Your Own Oyster Mushrooms in 5 Steps
1. *Find somewhere dark and humid.*
2. *Cut open the plastic on one end of the mushroom kit.*
3. *Cover the kit with a wet towel and lay the kit flat.*
4. *Spray water onto the opening twice a day to keep it moist.*
5. *Watch the mushrooms grow!*

It took me an hour to find somewhere to keep the kits. After inspecting the apartment, I decided to arrange them in a row under the bathroom sink. It seemed that all the kits I'd bought had the same instructions, which made the process quite straightforward.

By now, I wasn't sleeping at all at night. When the world around me calmed, I'd be wide awake, my muscles tense and my mind in chaos. Each night, I felt the need to do something; to take my mind off Bowen, Julia and the child who was dead. Naturally, I couldn't play the piano at three in the morning, so I was at a loss. I started going through cans of beer and bottles of wine at a much faster rate. When I realised I couldn't spend all my time drinking, I developed a habit of having meals during the night. Cooking and eating usually killed some more time, and around six or seven in the morning, I would fall asleep and not wake up again until mid-afternoon. As a result, I only saw my mother-in-law once that week.

It did not come as a surprise that my new schedule got me fired from a few of my teaching jobs, the homes where I taught on weekends. After failing to show up two days in a row, I was told by three mothers on the same day that I wasn't the right teacher for their children. The first two conversations went rather well, considering I was losing my job, but during the third phone call, I broke down in tears. I didn't ask her to give me another chance and I didn't even say sorry. I just cried. The poor mother began apologising to me, promising me that if I was going through any difficulties I was welcome to talk to her about them. I told her it was nothing.

With the extra time I had now, I started playing piano. For the first time since university, I wanted to work on a new piece. It wasn't that I'd never felt like playing for myself, but whenever I was in the mood, I played familiar pieces while following the scores. Now I wanted to find something I'd never played before and learn it well.

I went out and bought the sheet music for Clara Schumann's *Variations on a Theme by Robert Schumann*, op. 20. I've always loved Clara Schumann's compositions, but apart from *Drei Romanzen*, I'd never learned any of her works. Her relationship with Robert Schumann was something that, even as a child, I found to be flawlessly romantic, and it is reflected in many of their compositions. *Variations on a Theme by Robert Schumann* was one of her final compositions before she decided to focus on her performing career and her family. It was a birthday present for him, a few years before he died. They were so in love that even after his death, she spent the rest of her life performing and popularising his compositions.

I took my time going through each of the seven short movements. Though they're all variations on the same theme, they couldn't be more different in mood and texture. Some are fluid and subdued, like the original theme, others, like the fifth movement, are animated and tense – I'd even go so far as to say that it sounds angry. I wanted to learn them slowly.

Bowen was coming back in a couple of days. I found that the closer his return became, the less I was able to concentrate on playing and the more I wanted to leave him like he'd left Julia and the child she'd carried inside her.

One afternoon, while I was looking for a parking spot near Qian Gan Hutong, my phone rang with a number I didn't recognise. I picked up.

'How is he?' Julia asked.

She was using a different number, but from the first word I knew it was her.

'Is he happy?' she added.

'I'm not sure,' I said.

'Can you tell me more about him? I want to know what he's doing every day. Does he have any white hairs yet? Is he eating well? I'm only thirty-two and much of my hair has already turned grey. It's so ugly.'

I told her that in the years I had known Bowen, he had dedicated most of his waking hours to his work. Once, after he'd spent nine weekends in a row at the office, I asked him whether he really enjoyed his job that much. I had forgotten his response.

'He hates it,' Julia said. 'I know he does. He hated every job he ever had. But he has always worked hard at each and every one of them. He's one of those, you know? The kind of men who care too much about the things they despise.'

I found a spot by the street and reversed into it. Out of the car window, near a small square, I could see people ballroom dancing. Men and women were paired together while the three men who didn't have partners were standing to the side, waiting for their turn. The smog in the air was worse now that winter had arrived. Most of them were wearing masks.

A woman in a long brown coat passed by my car and obstructed my view for a moment. She had massive eyes that made her look like a deer. I watched her turn into Qian Gan Hutong.

'I haven't told him yet,' I said into the phone.

'I know,' she said. 'He would've called me.'

'Can you tell me,' I said. 'Is the soil red where you are?'

'The soil?'

'Yeah.'

'Some of it is red. Some of it is orange now.'

'Like on Mars?'

'I suppose it's like on Mars. The dust is not only near the river now, it's spread outwards to where people live. My roof is entirely covered in orange. This morning, it even got into my room and is now all over my lampshade. I spent the whole day dusting. On days when it's bad, you can't drive: you'd hardly be able to see the car in front of you.'

I pictured mountains, red mountains like blocks of raw beef, and dotting the slopes were houses with orange roofs.

'He's coming back from Shanghai in two days. I'll tell him then.' I hung up before she could respond.

*

'I won't be here much longer,' Bai Yu said halfway through the last page of *Rêverie*.

He had asked me to play this piece for the first time since the day we met. I had been hesitant, afraid that I'd fail him in my playing again, leading us back to where we'd begun – or even worse, that I'd find out that any progress we had made lived only in my imagination and he never wanted to see me again. I pretended not to hear him and continued playing.

'You shouldn't come again,' he said, withdrawing his hands.

I didn't stop. I felt like a pot of water being poured out. Each passing bar of the music reminded me of how close I was to being emptied completely. Too soon, the end of the piece came as softly as instructed on the page.

'Have you found it then?' I asked. 'That sound?'

'I don't believe I have,' he said. 'But something has changed since you and I met. Our fates have been melded together in a way that can never be undone. Like a game of tug of war, I'm afraid that I'm pulling you into my world, and I'm being drawn into yours. Soon we will both fall somewhere in the middle and lose touch as to what it is we're searching for. That is what terrifies me.'

'Is that such a bad thing?'

'If things were always either good or bad, then we would never feel anything.'

I grabbed his wrists and looked him in the eyes. They were dark brown. It was the first time I had ever reached out to touch him. His skin was the temperature of the room. It felt as though I wasn't touching anything at all.

'But nothing is ever so fixed, is it?' I said, grasping him harder. 'Haven't you considered that maybe the things you've been searching for are not lost, but that they have evolved into something else?'

I tried to secure his gaze, but he looked away. The late afternoon sun turned half of his face into the warm colour of pumpkin and the other half into an indistinct grey.

'Soon I will completely forget what I've been searching for,' he said. 'When that happens, I fear that the little part of me that's still left will not exist any more.'

'You haven't forgotten anything. Even if you wanted to, you wouldn't be able to.'

He didn't respond. I stood there, waiting for him to change his mind and ask me to stay, but he wouldn't move a muscle. I wondered how he could be so irresponsible, bringing me here with that letter and now telling me to leave again. I felt so useless and stupid to have allowed my heart to be dragged left and right across the ground like that. I thought about whether I'd ever be able to pretend none of this had happened and return to a life where every day was as predictable as the phases of the moon.

I closed the piano lid and draped the burgundy velvet cover over the instrument. There was no starting over. Thought might wish it so, but the heart is not a magical armour that can withstand anything; it is real and beating and capable of being wounded. Sometimes it can be as hard as a diamond and other times as frail as rice paper. I felt mine tear.

In the car, I pulled out the letter Bai Yu had sent me. I folded it into a paper airplane and for a second considered sending it flying out of the window, but ended up stuffing it back into my purse. I started the engine and drove around aimlessly until the low-fuel light came on. The clock read three in the morning. With nowhere else to go, I yielded and went back to what was supposed to be my home. When I walked into the apartment, Bowen's leather briefcase was by the door.

'You're back early,' I said, after I switched on the lights in the bedroom.

Bowen had been asleep and now he was annoyed. He pushed himself up with his elbows and squinted at me.

'Where have you been? What time is it? Turn off the light.'

I ignored him and went into the bathroom. I checked on the mushrooms in the basin cabinet. Nothing yet. That was to be expected. I sprayed some more water onto the bags, wetted the towel and placed it back on, and then closed the doors. I heard Bowen get out of bed to turn off the lights, after which he seemed to go back to sleep.

I had no idea what to do. I hadn't been prepared for this. I couldn't tell him about Julia. Not tonight. I shouldn't be so rash. Brushing my teeth and climbing into bed seemed out of the question too. I was disoriented, as though a cog in my engine had been put in the wrong place. It was as if I had only brought back a part of me and left the rest with Bai Yu. Words – too many of them – were flying into my head, but none pieced together into a sentence. Everything around me seemed off – the shower head, the toilet brush, the soap dispenser. They weren't the colour I remembered, or the material, or maybe they'd been moved. Did we even own a soap dispenser? Hadn't we always used bars? I couldn't recall.

I fled to the living room, turned on a recording of *Variations on a Theme by Robert Schumann*, and paced around in circles until the sun crawled out from behind the buildings, at which point I realised that the living room was no escape, as Bowen might wake up any second. I ran out and wandered around in the cold for what seemed like an eternity. The whole city felt like it was playing a game of musical chairs and I had become the person left standing. I toured the roads, desperate for a chair of my own. A small room. A back alley. Even a corner would suffice. Somewhere dark and quiet. The morning sun felt so glaringly sharp I could barely keep

my eyes open. It took me a few trips around the block
to scout a spot that was out of the light. Two men were
standing there, smoking, but I was too exhausted to
look for another place. I stayed there until I was sure
that Bowen had gone to work.

I'd forgotten to bring my keys, so my mother-in-law
had to open the door for me.

'I tried making breakfast for Bowen, but I couldn't
find the salt,' she said.

'It ran out a few days ago,' I said. 'It's so bright in the
living room.'

I rushed towards the bedroom without taking off my
shoes. 'I'm tired. I'm going to sleep.'

Before she responded, I already had the bedroom
door shut and locked behind me.

'Tired from what?' I heard her mutter in the living
room.

The bedroom window faced east, so the sun was
even stronger. I realised that I hadn't been awake at this
time of the day in a while. I drew the curtains and
coiled up in bed. The duvet was heavy and cool on my
body and the moment it touched me I was struck with
a sudden and overpowering sleepiness. I heard my
mother-in-law leave the apartment. I closed my eyes,
and almost immediately the whole world went silent, as
if all of it had been cast under a spell of unbroken
dreams.

I didn't wake up until it was dark again. Bowen hadn't come back yet. The sleepiness was entirely gone now and replaced with an excruciating hunger, as if my innards had been carved out and scraped clean. I sat on the sofa and ate a pack of graham crackers, which made me feel slightly better, and then I checked on the mushrooms again. I kneeled on the floor and inspected them closely, hoping to spot a pinhead or two sticking out, but there was still nothing.

Though I wasn't tired any more and I had managed to keep my hunger in check, my mind was still in a mess. In fact, the less my body demanded, the louder and more chaotic my thoughts became. I closed the basin cabinet door, found a notepad, sat on the bed and wrote down my options.

1. *Tell Bowen about Julia (and child), then return to life as usual.*
2. *Leave.*

I held the page between my fingers and stared at my handwriting. I mentally played out the potential scenarios. When Bowen came back, I could tell him that Julia had called, and then, like any wife and husband, we would sit down and formulate a plan together. He would apologise for not informing me before and I would be able to forgive him and hold his head to my chest and comfort him. From then on, we would have children of our own and this secret would be kept from them and buried with us forever.

I moved on to the second scenario. I pictured packing up my belongings – clothes, CDs, laptop, sheet music binders – and closing the door behind me. I would then throw the keys into the rubbish. But my train of thought ended there, crashed into a canyon. I couldn't imagine anything beyond that. Where would I run to? My parents? There was no way I could live with them, especially now that the life I'd given up the piano for wasn't the one I'd imagined after all.

I walked to the kitchen, poured myself a shot of whisky, and returned to my notebook. Going to my parents was out of the question. I killed the whisky and then decided to fetch the rest of the bottle.

By the time I finished my second glass, I had made up my mind not to run away. This was the life I had chosen and I had to bear its consequences. I couldn't reverse course at every obstacle. There were roads ahead and I had to walk them. I played the first option over and over in my mind. I rehearsed my words, my expression, how angry I was going to be, and how forgiving I was eventually going to become. Then I pictured the rest of our lives together; moving to a bigger place when we had children and growing old there. I thought about how normal and undisturbed our lives would be, like those happy and ordinary stories that never end up being told precisely because they are so happy and ordinary.

I opened Bowen's suitcase and fumbled through it. The navy suit jacket I had bought him for his birthday last year wasn't in there. I looked for the matching pants; they were sitting at the bottom of the suitcase. He must have taken the jacket to the dry cleaner. Realising that I had no intention of unpacking for him, I zipped up the suitcase and rolled it to the corner of the room.

It was getting late now and I couldn't hear my mother-in-law at all. What if she never came back? Maybe she'd told Bowen about how disappointed she was in me and had asked him to buy her a ticket to Yunnan this afternoon. In so doing she would've denied me the chance to send her off at the airport like a good daughter-in-law. Was that why Bowen still hadn't come home? Normally, he'd call to say if he was going to be late.

I went into the dark living room. When I saw a yellow light spilling from under my mother-in-law's door, a sense of relief washed over me. It gave me the courage I needed to call Bowen.

He picked up after a few rings. Again, there were noises in the background. He wasn't at the office. I asked him what he was doing.

'I'm having dinner with my co-workers,' he said. 'Our boss is here too.'

Whenever he mentioned that he was with his boss, I knew we wouldn't be able to talk long.

'Come back soon,' I said. 'I have things to speak with you about.'

'Let's leave it for tomorrow. I can't go home before the boss. He's had a few drinks and doesn't look like he's going to stop anytime soon. Go to bed without me.'

He would most likely rush home if I mentioned that Julia had called, I thought. Would he even recognise the name Julia?

I heard someone call to him.

He moved his phone away from his lips and said to the other person, 'Please hold on one minute, my *fu ren* is on the phone.'

I heard the others laughing. I knew what amused them. Bowen had always been so proper that even I would find it comical at times. He never referred to me as his *lao po*, favouring the word *fu ren*. I knew that using a more formal word to refer to his wife made him feel tasteful and reserved, and it wasn't even uncommon, but to me, the word ignored all the intimacies of a marriage. It made me feel like nothing more than a name on a certificate.

'Is Wang Xiao with you?' I asked.

'He went home after work.'

'Then why did you have to stay?'

I regretted asking that the moment it came out of my

mouth. I didn't want to hear him talk about his promotion again and how essential this meal was to fulfilling
his ambitions.

But, unexpectedly, he said, 'I can come back soon.
You sound troubled.'

'It's nothing,' I heard myself respond instantly. 'I
must just be tired. You know what? You should get back
to dinner.'

I didn't know why I couldn't tell him to come home
and explain the things he had kept from me. I let my
hand holding the phone slide onto my lap and leaned
my head back, waiting for him to hang up.

But after a moment, from the muffled and muted
sounds of the receiver, I heard him say, 'Are you sure?'

These three words brushed against my skin as if they
were cashmere, momentarily giving me the illusion
of warmth. My chest began to ache, and soon the
pain travelled upwards into my head. There must've
been many moments of tenderness between us. How
many had gone unnoticed, and how many had been
forgotten?

'It's nothing, really,' I said. 'I just wanted to ask you
what you think of the name Julia.'

'What?'

I couldn't tell whether he understood what I was
implying or whether he was simply confused by my
question.

'Maybe for our future daughter, you know? We can give her an English name. Send her to school in America. Or England.'

He didn't respond.

'Think about it, will you?' I said and hung up the phone.

Not long ago I'd wanted to know the truth. My naiveté had led me to believe that if only we'd shared the truth, our hearts would be brought together. Now, the truth only made the unsurpassable distance between us clearer than ever. I curled up on the couch and waited all night, but Bowen didn't come back.

The sun had not set entirely, but the living room was already dark. Bowen had called earlier and said that he'd stayed at a hotel, having had a little too much to drink. I paused in the middle of practising and switched on the floor lamp next to the piano. As I was doing this, my mother-in-law came out from her room with a bag of walnuts, sat on the sofa and began cracking the shells with a small hammer.

'Can you come sit with me for a bit?' she asked. 'Bring that jar with you.'

She pointed towards a row of glass jars sitting on the window sill, each containing a different type of nut kernel. I fetched the half-empty walnut jar and made my way to the sofa.

'I'll do it,' I said, taking the hammer from her.

She gave a smile that was too polite, as if by accept-
ing my gesture, she now owed me more than she could
ever give back. While Bowen was away, I had started to
see that she was carrying guilt with her like a basket of
stones. After many years, the stones' edges had lost
their sharpness, but the weight of them remained. No
person could balance this load on their shoulders without becoming bruised. She felt unworthy of kindness
even as she needed it more and more.

She took out an envelope from her cardigan pocket
and placed it on the coffee table.

'This is for you,' she said. 'I've noticed that you're
teaching less these days.'

I finished cracking the nut I had in my hand and
dropped the kernel into the jar. I brushed the scraps off
my hands before taking the envelope and placing it
back in her cardigan pocket.

'We have enough,' I said. 'You keep this.'

'I want to help—'

'There's no need.'

We both stared at the walnuts.

'Bowen had a son,' I said. 'With his previous wife.'

My voice sounded so composed that I wasn't even
sure I'd said anything. But my mother-in-law's eyes,
which nowadays rarely ever looked straight at me, were
now locked onto mine.

'Where? Where is he?' she asked.

She turned her body to face me, running her knee

into the table. A few walnuts rolled off. I bent over to pick up them up, one by one.

'He didn't want to keep the child,' I said.

She wanted to ask something else but she remained silent. She must have decided that she couldn't stand to know more. When I looked up, her face was cracked and dry like the walnut shells on the table, as though she'd already lived the rest of her life. I couldn't bring myself to tell her that the child was no longer alive.

She took out the envelope again, placed it on my lap, and went back into her room.

I'd been waiting all evening until Bowen finally came home. He greeted me and apologised for staying at a hotel. He hadn't wanted to interrupt my sleep, he said. He went into his mother's room while I waited in the living room, troubled by the possibility that she'd tell him about our conversation earlier. But she didn't seem to have mentioned anything. After he came out, we chatted for a while on the sofa, recounting the past few months, which mostly involved him telling me about Munich.

Before going to bed, while he was unpacking his suitcase, I decided that it was a good time to talk to him.

'Julia called me,' I said. 'I don't know her by any other name. You were married to her before.'

He didn't look at me.

'What did she say?' he asked.

I picked my words carefully.

'She said you had a child.'

He took out his electric shaver and threw it onto the bed.

'She said she kept the baby even though you didn't want to,' I said.

He continued fumbling through his suitcase, sorting out the shirts that needed washing and flattening out the rest with his hands before hanging them up in the closet.

Afraid that if I let the room fall silent, I'd never be able to finish, I kept talking.

'She wanted me to tell you that an orange dust appeared all over your home town,' I said. 'It landed on the surface of the river. The child was playing there.'

I didn't know how to tell him that his son was dead, just as I couldn't tell his mother. The words wouldn't come out of my mouth. I remembered Julia's voice over the phone. *Our child drowned*, she had said. As I looked for the right words to say to Bowen, I realised that there were none. I could repeat Julia's words or I could attempt to tell him less directly, but either way, the meaning would be the same.

I couldn't find a way, either, to ask him why he hadn't wanted to keep the child; whether it had anything to do with losing his sister; and how it felt to suffer the loss of his son all over again. I didn't know how to reach into his heart and pull out the truth without ripping a hole through it. Looking at him, still dressed in the suit that he wore everyday like armour, I saw the man beneath – the one who had fled from his past only to see it grow and catch up with him one day.

Today, I decided, was not going to be that day.

'You should speak with her,' I finally said. 'I can give you her number.'

He hung up the last shirt, took the shaver from the bed and went to brush his teeth, without saying a word. I wrote down Julia's number on a piece of paper and placed it on the nightstand. While he was still in the bathroom, I packed a change of clothes in a knapsack and left.

I drove to Nini's place. She was still up. When I told her that I wanted to stay with her for the night, she didn't ask me why and told me that I was welcome to use her mother's bedroom. The last time I had been in that room was when Nini's mother was still alive. Since then, Nini had kept the door closed and never once had it occurred to me to push it open and take a look.

'I can sleep on the couch,' I told her.

'She wouldn't let me do that to you.' Nini smiled. 'She liked you so much.'

Nini held my wrist while she gently turned the knob and pushed open the door as though someone still lived in there and might've been sleeping.

'It's dusty in here,' she said. 'If you want to stay longer, we can clean up tomorrow.'

She fetched a set of blankets from the closet and placed them at the end of the bed. I thanked her.

'Don't mention it. I'm sure married life isn't always easy.'

I laughed. 'You can't even imagine.'

'Oh, of course I can! That's why I've stayed away from it all this time.'

She kicked her slippers to me. 'Here, take these for now. I'll find some more tomorrow. I was just about to go to bed. I have to be at the salon at eight.'

I fell asleep for an hour, waking again at midnight. Even though that hour was all the rest I'd had in more than a day, I was wide awake, like a bat. It had been raining. I made myself a cup of instant noodles and brought it to the bedroom. Everything in the room was kept the same, and despite what Nini had said, there wasn't any dust. It actually looked rather clean compared to the rest of the apartment. There was a small shelf with a handful of old books – one on birds, three cookbooks, a few pieces of clarinet sheet music and some Sanmao novels. Nini's mother had sold her desk long ago to make room for a piano, which she'd bought second-hand from their neighbour so that she could learn to play duets with Nini. It didn't take her long to realise that it was far more difficult than she'd imagined, so I ended up being the person who used the piano the most.

After I finished my noodles, I lay in bed and watched the rain intensify. It should have snowed already by this time of the year. The harder I concentrated on the sounds, the quieter the world became, the raindrops only adding to the silence. It was kind of like Bai Yu's music, I thought. Eventually, I could sleep again. When I woke up, the orange mushroom was on my bed.

'It's you again,' the mushroom said.

It was massive, just like an open umbrella. The cap was much flatter than I'd remembered. It was growing out from the footboard of the bed and the way its stem curved made it seem as if it was sitting on the wooden plank. I sat up and touched it. The cap felt like the surface of a balloon. I looked around. This time, perhaps because the mushroom was bigger and glowed brighter, I could make out the shape of the room, its walls now bare, with a door in the wall to the left of me.

'Forget it,' the mushroom said. 'That exit is blocked.'

I ignored it and went straight for the door, but I couldn't find a knob. I grabbed the edge and tried pulling. It wouldn't even budge. Then I kicked it as hard as I could, and when that didn't work, I returned to bed and sat facing the mushroom.

'Do you remember me?' it said.

'It's hard to forget fungus that can talk.'

'Then you must remember that I'm not a mushroom. What kind do you think I am? Oyster? Portobello?'

'Now that you mention it, a giant portobello looks about right.'

'If that helps you make sense of me, then think of me however you want.'

'Maybe *you* can help me make sense of this,' I said. 'I just need to fall asleep to get out of here, right?'

'Does it frighten you? To be in here?'

Even though the mushroom was much bigger, I still couldn't tell where the voice was coming from. It certainly didn't have a mouth. Maybe it was talking with its gills, but that was just a guess.

'I suppose it does worry me that I can't seem to leave when I want to,' I said.

The bedsheets were damp and the temperature felt too warm for winter. Though subtle, the air had the same musky smell from before, combined with something slightly sour. My T-shirt stuck to my skin. Beads of water and sweat were forming on my forehead.

'What are you exactly?' I asked.

The mushroom couldn't have any expressions, but it seemed to me as if it was meditating on my question.

'Think of me as a ghost,' it eventually said.

'This isn't what I pictured ghosts as looking like.'

'Conceptually, I'm more similar to ghosts than mushrooms.'

For obvious reasons, I had a hard time believing that. Its high-pitched voice now took on a hint of melancholy, as though it couldn't put into words what it really was. To compare itself with a ghost meant that it had to abandon something important in its essence, like a raindrop that fell through the air knowing that it would lose its shape forever upon hitting the ground.

'So you were once alive?' I asked. 'And now you're dead. Turned into a spirit.'

'Very loosely speaking, something like that.'

It was too hot to get back under the covers, so I lay over them and tried to fall asleep like I had the last time, but I was so awake I couldn't even keep my eyes shut. I decided to hum the melody of Nocturne in E-flat major, which had always worked to put me to sleep when I was little.

'What is that?' the mushroom ghost said.

I stopped. 'The music? It's Chopin.'

There was no way a mushroom ghost would know Chopin, though the situation was strange enough that anything could happen.

'Keep going,' it said.

So I did. I went through the whole piece and, following the mushroom ghost's request for more, I did Nocturne in B-flat minor too.

'I'm going to try the door again,' I said when I finished.

I walked to the door and put my ear on it. For a moment, I thought I heard someone speaking, so I pressed harder into the wood to listen. But I must have been imagining things. There was only dead silence.

When I turned round, the mushroom ghost was gone and the room was normal again. Behind me now, the door to the living room had been left ajar. I went over to the piano and pressed my hand onto the lid, leaving a handprint on the glossy black trim.

The curtains didn't do much to keep the city lights out, so I drew them open. The rain had turned into snow and the streets were crusted with a thin layer of white. Bit by bit, the humidity in the room subsided.

SNOW

I had three missed calls from Bowen. Whenever he couldn't get hold of me, he would call exactly three times in quick succession, after which he'd wait for me to respond without trying again. My pyjamas looked like I'd jumped into a swimming pool during the night, so I had to take a shower. Nini was already awake. She was eating grapes out of a bag and pouring instant coffee into a thermal bottle.

'I have milk in the fridge,' she said. 'I'll leave the key here in case you want to go out.'

She pointed to the kitchen counter. There was a single key without a keyring. I couldn't remember the last time I'd seen someone keep their keys like that. I asked her if I could stay another night or two and she told me that I could use the room for as long as I wanted.

'You should stay forever,' she added, smiling. 'If you cook every day, I promise I'll finally stop eating instant noodles.'

'How about I cook you a nice breakfast of instant

noodles? See, you first have to boil water. You know how to boil water? You pour water into the kettle—'

She threw a grape at me. I blocked it with my arm and it fell to the ground. I bent over and picked it up.

'Toss it,' she said. 'I'll catch it with my mouth.'

'It's dirty,' I said. 'And you're not eight years old.'

I rinsed the grape under the tap, gave it to her and went into the bathroom. In the shower, I thought about reminding Nini to take an umbrella in case the temperature went up during the day and the snow turned into rain again, knowing that there was no way she'd think of that herself. In a way, she *is* like a child. I imagined what might have been going through her mother's mind before she died. She must have been so worried about her daughter, remembering all the times she could've taught Nini to cook but didn't.

When I came out of the shower, Nini had left for work. The grapes were on the counter so I ate a few and put them away in the refrigerator. I drank some milk, got changed and headed towards the supermarket. A young man wearing a military coat was organising shopping carts at the entrance and pushing them into one another to form a row. When he saw me, he let go of the cart in his hand and opened the glass door for me. Close up, he smelled like winter – powdery, a little salty.

When I thanked him, he said, with an eager smile, 'Go on, go on, it's cold out here.'

It wasn't much better inside. Somebody must've
decided that they could save money on cooling the
refrigerators if they kept the entire place like one. Not
wanting to stay too long, I quickly decided to make
zhajiang noodles, so I grabbed some noodles, cucum-
bers, minced pork, sweet sauce and bean paste. I also
added a bag of apples and a carton of eggs to my basket.
The cashier wore a red down coat and a blue scarf. Her
cheeks were almost the same colour as her coat. While
I was counting money, she rubbed her hands together
and blew into them.

Before going back, I drove to Bai Yu's place. I stood
outside the gate, waiting for something to happen.
Maybe he'd come out. What if he had to go to the
supermarket as well? After ten minutes or so, I couldn't
stand the cold any more, so I knocked on the gate. Since
I'd been told explicitly not to come any more, I refrained
from walking in like I had always done, and even when
nobody answered, I knocked a few more times. He was
only two walls away from me, but the closer I was to
him, the more overwhelming his absence became.

I thought about the possibility that he wasn't there,
and that behind the gate was an empty house with no
traces of him ever having been there. What if he had
just been a product of my imagination? I decided I had
to make sure that he did still exist. Right when I was
about to open the gate, a woman walked up beside me.
She faced the gate and looked straight at it, as if her

eyes were able to penetrate the wood and she was watching everything inside that I couldn't see. This made me uneasy, even a little jealous. She wore a long umber coat and a beret in a darker shade of brown. Her tall boots were brown too and disappeared under her coat. Vapour was coming out from between her slightly opened lips, which were glazed with a rosy tint. She looked familiar.

I stepped aside, allowing her to pass if she wished to, but she remained still as a stick and stared at the gate. Was she a friend of his? Why wasn't she going in? Had she come to the wrong address? With her gloved hands, she brushed some snow off the heads of the stone lion dogs at the entrance and walked away. As she moved down the narrow street, she didn't even turn her head to look at any of the other gates she passed.

Watching her walk away, I remembered that I'd seen her before, on the night I sat in my car watching people ballroom dancing. Julia had been on the phone. The woman had walked into Qian Gan Hutong back then. Maybe she was a neighbour, I thought. If so, did she know Bai Yu? Why had I assumed that I was the only one who knew he was living here?

I pushed my way inside. There weren't any footsteps in the snow. The courtyard was a perfect white square, like a giant handkerchief. I took a deep breath and walked right down the middle towards the house.

I leaned on the door.

'Bai Yu?' I called.

After a moment, the door opened with a squeak and he was behind it. I was relieved.

He moved aside to let me in. He didn't seem like he was going to say anything, so I didn't either. Both of us turned left into the piano room. He sat down on the bench and lay his fingers over the keys. He didn't press them down to make a sound or even move them, and before I was able to think it through, I was behind him with my fingers spread over his. His body tensed and I couldn't feel him breathing. I pushed my left ring finger down, B flat, then my middle finger, C, followed by D, and then as I reached for the next key, he gently lay his other hand on mine as though he was muffling the vibrations of a drum. It lasted just a second before he wasn't touching me any more and had stood up.

'Have you ever read Oscar Wilde?' he asked.

I shook my head.

'An old friend of mine used to quote him a lot. He said to live is the rarest thing in the world. Most people only exist.'

He walked away from the bench and stood next to the piano. I could see his body relax a little, as if that was where he belonged.

'Why have you come?' he asked.

I ran a few responses through my head. Most of them would've been lies.

'I was listening to a recording of myself,' I decided to

say. 'But it felt like nobody was playing and the sounds were just there, like they'd always been there and someone just turned up the volume knob.'

'How can you be sure, then,' he said, 'that it was you playing?'

'I suppose I can't be sure,' I said. 'Do you still listen to your own recordings?'

'I don't need to any more.'

'The one thing more important than playing is to listen to yourself play. That's what I always tell my students. I like listening to myself play when I'm with you. So, to answer your question, I came here because I want to be where you are.'

Briefly, I saw an expression I'd never seen on him before – somewhat embarrassed, somewhat angry.

'Tell me,' he said in a louder voice than I'd ever heard him use. 'Do you think Oscar Wilde considered how someone can attempt to live if that person never existed? If I can't even feel my existence, how could I possibly think about living? Now, do you still want to be where I am?'

'But you exist,' I said. 'I know it. I've heard it.'

'What you heard were empty sounds. They're not real.'

'Emptiness can be real.'

I wished there was a way for him to understand that he was more than just a shadow that emerged and faded with the light, and if he denied his existence, then he'd also be rejecting the part of me that had become so deeply entwined with him. And I couldn't allow him to reduce that part of me to nothing but a fantasy. I so desperately wanted to ask him why was it that we were both in pain, yet there was nothing we could do to comfort one another?

The first time I saw him, I really did question whether he was real or if I'd just gone mad. He felt like a strange dream back then, one that called for nothing more than a head scratch upon waking up. But even a dream would become real if you come back to it often enough.

He was much too preoccupied with his own thoughts for any of my words to reach him. Was every day for him like my listening to my own recording? Maybe I could've been more convincing if I didn't understand him at all. Being capable of recognising that feeling, even if only vaguely, made it difficult for me to go further.

'I've never told you much about myself, have I?' I said. 'My father is a pianist. Maybe you've heard of him. His name is Song Qianshi. Qian from "thousand", shi as in "stones". It's his stage name, but it might as well be his actual name since it's the only one he ever uses. My mother is a housewife. My husband sells cars. He thinks his job is more than that, but when you boil it down, he's a car salesman. We don't have children. Um . . . let's see . . . what else . . .'

I knew Bai Yu probably didn't care about any of this, but I went on.

'Oh, my mother-in-law lives with us. She wants a grandchild, but my husband doesn't. Though, actually, he had a child with a previous wife. I found out recently. The child drowned in a river. I couldn't tell him.'

Bai Yu stared right at me with a painful coldness. It drove me to look away. Not knowing what to do with my body, I sat down and played a B-flat minor chord. If I had a favorite chord, this would be it. My mother always used to ask me, 'Can you play that chord? The one I like. The one that sounds like it's been snowing all winter.' Then she would pause whatever she was doing and tell me to play the entire scale. Sometimes, I would improvise a melody to go with it – a mini song in her favourite key.

'Do you ever leave this house?' I asked.

'I have to wait here,' Bai Yu said.

'For what?'

'Someone from the past.'

I let the chord drag on until it was gone.

'Hey, what about those mushrooms?' I asked. 'I started growing my own.'

'I'm glad you liked them, but I don't have any more for you. They've stopped coming for me too.'

My phone rang.

'That's not what I meant,' I said as I unzipped my jacket pocket and took my phone out.

It was from an unknown number. Bai Yu shifted his glance out of the window, signalling to me that it was all right for me to take the call.

'Your car is blocking the entrance of the alley,' a man's voice said. 'I can't get to my house.'

I apologised a few times while trying to remember how I'd parked my car. I told the man I'd be out there in a second. With a maddened mumble, he said, 'Hurry up.'

Bai Yu was still facing the window. Besides the few minutes of sunlight in the morning, it had mostly been overcast all day, as though the sky had been paused at dusk. I told him I had to go and he walked me to the door. I didn't hear him lock it behind me.

Outside the courtyard, as I was heading towards the entrance of the alleyway, I saw that a small crowd had gathered there. There was an old man, a pregnant woman accompanied by another woman whose face resembled an otter's, some other people I can't remember and a red car.

'Is this your car?' the otter said to me as I ran towards them.

'I'm sorry. I thought I'd parked it properly.'

'Don't you have any respect?' the otter said. 'Does driving a BMW give you the right to park like a gangster?'

'It's my husband's company car. He works at BMW. I'm sorry.'

I wanted to tell her that we weren't the type of family that could afford this car at full price. On everyday occasions, Bowen still preferred to drive our old Toyota. Only when he had to represent the company would we switch cars for the day. I, however, enjoyed the luxury. It meant that other cars on the street would refrain from driving too close to me for fear of scraping my car and having to pay for the repairs.

'She's pregnant,' the otter continued, pointing towards the pregnant lady, as if her giant belly bulging out didn't make it obvious enough. 'What if there's an emergency and she needs to go to the hospital? Your phone number is written so small. We could barely read it.' Then she pointed towards the old man. 'And he's old. You can't expect him to drive through this tiny space you left for him. Especially on a snowy day like today.'

'I'm old,' the old man repeated after the otter.

His expression was so begrudging, you'd believe it if he said I'd murdered his family. The rest of the crowd nodded like piano hammers.

I walked behind the car and looked at the space I'd left. It wasn't the most generous, and I admit that I could've inched a little further forward, but it was certainly wide enough for his car to drive through. A younger man stepped up to me from the crowd with an awkward smile.

'Please understand,' he said. 'It's difficult for old people to manoeuvre through small spaces.'

I lied and said that I'd only stopped by to drop off some things and hadn't expected to stay long. I told them I was leaving, upon which the crowd dissipated, the old man stepped into his car and the younger one started directing me out of there, perhaps because he'd felt embarrassed by the whole scene.

While driving, I couldn't relax at all. I almost ran into a woman riding a yellow rental bike. For the life of me, I couldn't imagine Bai Yu living on the same street as that crowd of people. Did they even know that a few houses down the road lived the once-famous piano prodigy? An image came to my mind. It was summer and the otter was watching TV while biting off the last chunks of flesh around the core of a pear. Sailing in through the window were sounds of me playing *Swallows* with Bai Yu. The otter turned up the TV's volume and threw the pear core into the rubbish bin.

When I got back to Nini's, I made the zhajiang sauce and stored it in a container. A few hours later, Nini came through the door and, upon smelling the sauce, scooped a spoonful and stuffed it into her mouth.

'Hey, why don't we open a restaurant,' she joked.

I grabbed the container from her. 'Wait for the noodles.'

She wiped the dining table. While we ate, I told her about my parking incident. She laughed throughout the whole story, which made me feel better.

As she slurped the last few strands of noodles into

her mouth, she asked me, 'Why were you trying to drive in the tiny hutongs anyway?'

'I went to see a friend.'

'You have other friends?'

'Of course I do. So where's your clarinet? You want to play something together?'

'I very much don't want to. Give me a break. I had to wash twenty-six stinky heads today.'

'You count how many people you wash?'

'It helps me keep track of time.'

'Come on, just one piece.'

She slid down in the chair like an eel and right when she was about to hit the floor, she pushed herself up.

'Fine. But don't make fun of me.' She went into her room and came back with her clarinet.

Even though the piano lid had been down, there was a layer of dust on the keys. I brushed it off with a dry towel and played a few notes. It was horrendously out of tune – my father would've called it a neglected concubine – but I didn't mind so much.

'Oh dear, that piano sounds like it should be thrown out the window,' Nini said.

'Do you remember any pieces?'

'Let's see what I have.'

She tapped on my back to indicate that she needed to access the storage compartment of the bench. I stood up. She sifted through and pulled out a book from the middle of the pile and handed it to me.

'What about Brahms?' she said while sucking on a reed.

I flipped through the titles and picked out the first movement of the Sonata in F minor. I've always liked Brahms's clarinet sonatas, particularly because if he hadn't met Mühlfeld and fallen in love with his performance, Brahms might have retired forever, and that is a sad thought.

'I only have one copy, so we'll have to share,' Nini said.

We played at a slower tempo than indicated since neither of us was familiar with the piece any more. We had hiccups, but we didn't care and not once did we stop to correct anything. On occasion, I looked over at Nini's hands, which were dry and chapped. The skin around her knuckles was a soft red. When she moved her fingers, I could see where her veins intersected with her bones like the knotted trunk of a wisteria.

My mother always kept a jar of hand cream by the sink for me and my father. Once, while shopping together, she talked to Nini's mother about the importance of hands to musicians, after which Nini's mother bought a tube of cream and placed it on Nini's music stand. Every time I went to their place, I remember Nini removing the tube from the stand to make space for the sheet music and putting it back again after we were done. Years passed and the weight of the pink tube had remained the same.

When we arrived at the end of the sonata, I looked over at the music stand that was in the corner of the room. The tube of cream wasn't there any more.

Later that evening, little Shaobo's father called to cancel the lesson that was scheduled for the next day. Little Shaobo was sick, he said. The boy had come down with a fever and had to go to the hospital.

'Would you like to speak with him?' his father asked hesitantly. 'That should cheer him up a bit.'

I agreed. He passed the phone to his son and whispered, 'It's Ms Song. She wants you to get better soon so that you can play piano together again!'

'I'm sad we have to miss our lesson tomorrow,' I said as lovingly as I could. 'But when you are well again, I have a new piece for you! Isn't that exciting?'

Little Shaobo gave a weak giggle while Nini looked at me with a teasing grin.

'Ms Song,' he said, 'I didn't like the piano at first, but now I like it. I also like you!'

'That's wonderful to hear. Do you know what I'd like?'

'What?'

'I'd like you to get a lot of rest so that I can see you soon!'

'What about the piano? Do you like the piano?'

I sighed. This boy really had a talent for asking difficult questions. It wasn't that I'd never thought about the answer to this particular one. As a matter of fact, it was something that'd been on my mind every day for years. So I knew all too well that it was impossible to answer. I should tell him that I couldn't like or dislike something that, arguably, had been bigger than my life itself. It carried with it something that belonged to my father, my mother, Nini and so many others around me. The matter wasn't so simple. Were there people who could say with unwavering certainty that they liked what they lived for, even on days when they wanted to destroy all of it? If such people existed, then I wouldn't hesitate to throw myself away and become one of them.

I told little Shaobo that I would only answer his question after he got well again. He accepted my pretence and said goodnight before handing the phone back to his father.

Since my lesson was cancelled and Nini didn't have work the following day, the two of us felt no guilt about staying up late. It was past midnight and we'd each had a few bottles of beer. Nini asked about my mother-in-law and how I'd been coping living together with her. I filled her in with the past few months of my life. I kept Bai Yu a secret and focused only on the things I'd found out about Bowen.

'Do you think he's called Julia yet?' she asked.

I shook my head.

'You can't really blame her, can you?'

I shook my head again.

'So, are you going to go back and pretend like you don't know anything?' She wedged open a beer bottle with a lighter that had come out of nowhere and handed it to me.

I took a large gulp from the bottle and felt the bubbles push down my throat like pills.

'I've been thinking about it,' I said. 'Imagining what it would be like if I just forgot everything and lived a life in peace, had kids, raised them, grew old, all of that.' I took another sip. The beer made my stomach cold. 'But then I can't help but think, if I can already watch each day of my life play out like an old recording, am I still alive?'

Both of us reflected on my words.

Nini was the first to speak again. 'How about something stronger?' She went to the dining table and brought back two empty glasses and a bottle of Jack Daniel's. She popped open the cap and poured us each a drink.

'Last week,' she said, 'a girl who works with me at the salon punched the mirror in our bathroom. No one saw it coming. She's never been the most joyful, but she is sweet and one of the more helpful people around the place. Usually you can tell the kind of person who expresses anger with physical violence, you know? But with her, I couldn't sense anything like that. On top of it all, she's tiny. Her hands are so small. I wouldn't even think she had the strength to punch through a mirror. She came to Beijing a few years ago and I know she doesn't have much money, so part of the reason why she's so skinny is that she isn't eating well at all. She's working several jobs at once, which must be stressful, but whenever she talked about it, it seemed like she wasn't too bothered by it.'

I was around twelve when I first experienced an anger so overpowering that I wanted to hit something. It was the only time that my anger manifested itself in something physical. I banged my fists on the refrigerator while my mother watched me with a doting smile, which only fuelled my fury even more. It was a sizzling summer afternoon – a suitable day to get heated. My mother had just cooked lunch and I could feel the grease in the air bonding to my skin. The backs of my bare thighs were stuck to the chair in our kitchen. I was supposed to go to my piano lesson, but an urge to rebel coiled and tightened around my chest like a python. My parents wouldn't let me have my way, so I still ended up braving the heat and trudging to my piano teacher's home across town. I remember that moment like it was yesterday, when my small body couldn't contain the extent of my emotions any more, driving me to look for another vessel to share them with.

Now that I think about it, I don't recall ever having felt anger before that. I'd experienced frustration in many instances. There were even times I'd pretended to be angry, but true anger had been foreign to me. What I felt then was new – it was exciting.

'It's crazy how everybody suddenly became so afraid of her,' Nini continued. 'Even our boss was too scared to fire her after that. A few days ago, when it was just the two of us cleaning up after work, I asked her what was wrong. She told me that she'd snuck home some hair dye from the salon, but her husband wouldn't help her dye her hair. Apparently, he thought dyeing her hair would make her seem too pretentious. She was really angry.'

'What colour?' I asked.

'Huh?'

'What colour did she want to dye her hair?'

'Oh. Chestnut, I think.'

'Hmm.'

Nini drank from her glass before continuing.

'Anyway, today, after lunch, while sweeping the hair on the ground, out of nowhere she just broke down crying. In front of customers and everyone. I took her into the bathroom and she just kept pointing into the mirror and saying, "That's not me, that's not me. I wasn't born to be like this." I asked her, "What do you mean?" and she said, "How could you call that a woman?"'

'What happened afterwards?' I asked.

'She got fired.'

We emptied our glasses and Nini said that she was going to sleep. My head was spinning, so I curled up and closed my eyes. I wasn't sure whether I was thinking or dreaming, but I thought I saw little Shaobo lying in bed, feverish, cheeks all red, with a needle up his arm. The next moment, he was dead and in his place was Bowen's child, a sheet covering his body. I reached out to touch the sheet and under my hands was the white snow in Bai Yu's courtyard.

The next afternoon, I decided to go home. Nini told me that I could come back anytime. We ate the rest of the zhajiang noodles for dinner and at around eight in the evening, when I thought Bowen was about to get off work, I packed my things and drove back to our apartment.

My mother-in-law was in the living room when I walked in the door. Upon seeing me, she didn't say anything, turned off the TV and dragged herself into her bedroom like a fly with a broken wing. I couldn't sense any emotion from her and saw only the brutality of age; how growing old was not a process but something that happened between one instant and the next.

I made no effort to talk to her either, and went into our bathroom to check on the mushrooms. The bags were dry and nothing had grown, so I sprayed some more water on them and let them be. An hour later, Bowen came back so drunk that he looked like a completely different person. His clothes were still impeccably neat, but his eyes looked as though someone had tried to carve them out. His eyeballs and the skin around them were all red and the lids drooped like they were melting. The first thing that occurred to me was how much he resembled his elderly mother. Wang Xiao was with him. He forced a nervous smile when he saw me. He tried to move Bowen to the couch, but Bowen leaned against the wall and started to untie his shoelaces, only to lose his balance and fall on the floor.

'Ow!' he shouted.

Making no effort to get up, he sat at the entranceway like a stray dog on the road. He was still wrestling with his shoes when I went over and tried pulling him up by the arm.

'I didn't know you were coming back,' he said. 'I can't untie this.'

'I'm sorry,' Wang Xiao said. 'I should've stopped him. It got a little out of hand.'

I took Bowen's shoes off for him, but he still refused to get up from the floor.

I glanced over at Wang Xiao, who didn't seem like he was going to leave just yet.

'I want to talk to you,' I said to Bowen.

He made an OK sign with his hand.

'Fine,' I said, and leaned against the shoe cabinet. 'We can talk here.'

From above, he looked small and fragile. It pained me to see him unable to hold his head up. He tried to focus his eyes on mine but couldn't.

I couldn't wait for Wang Xiao to leave. The words shot up from my stomach like steam escaping a water boiler. Before I knew it, they'd come out already.

'Why didn't you tell me?' I asked. 'About your child?'

'It doesn't matter,' Bowen said.

'How can it not matter?'

Tears started forming in my eyes and all I wanted to do was inhale a lungful of the cold air outside. The impulse to leave and avoid an argument made me choke on my saliva. I forced myself to stay put.

'You just can't seem to get over the whole children thing, can you?' he said, grinning as if it was a funny joke.

Then, in a flash, he looked sober again, more than ever, and his eyes stared right into mine as if he was begging for his life. It was with that expression that he said to me, 'I don't ever want to have children.'

Wang Xiao nudged him with his elbow, but Bowen was too drunk to notice. I turned away, darted into the bedroom, opened the closet and stared at my clothes. I wanted to pack everything and get out of there. Drive to a place where nobody could find me. This time, I wouldn't return. I could erase all my thoughts for a moment, pretend my mind didn't exist; focus on the sounds of birds. When was the last time I'd turned off my thoughts? Is that even possible? How do we endure living with a mind that can't stop, starting the moment we're born until the day we die?

I heard Wang Xiao say to Bowen, 'Song Yan is upset. Get up. This is your family.'

Wang Xiao was right. This was my home. I had to make one last attempt to stay. I returned to the living room, where Bowen was still sitting bent over on the floor, his head rolling from one knee to another. When he heard me, he twisted his neck sideways to look at me, forehead still touching his legs. Wang Xiao shifted uncomfortably. I wanted to tell him that he didn't have to be embarrassed. I was the one who should feel ashamed.

'Come here,' Bowen said, beckoning with his hand. 'Let me show you something.'

He straightened up a bit, took out his phone and clicked on a link that he'd saved. It led to an article titled 'Yunnan's Red Lands Covered in Orange' and was accompanied by an aerial photo of a town. The image showed an orange river running along the side, orange trees scattered all around, and orange houses next to one another. Near the river, there were orange dust clouds in the air.

Bowen pointed at his phone.

'I'm never going back there.' He sounded as if he was trying to convince himself. 'Look at that.'

Then he hurled his phone across the living room into his mother's door. Upon hitting the wooden floor, the phone shattered. Wide-eyed, Wang Xiao and I looked at each other.

'Did you hear that, Ma?' Bowen yelled. 'I'm never going back there!'

He pointed at me. 'She wants a child. You want a grandson. All of you want me to have children. But I don't have to listen to any of you. It's *my* decision to make.'

Then he pointed to Wang Xiao.

'And he . . . Well, I'm sure he wants a child too.'

Turning back to face his mother's room, he shouted, 'You have no right to talk about family!'

My mother-in-law opened the door and stood there watching her son repeat the last sentence over and over again. Her eyes were lustrous with tears, but she didn't let a single one escape. When Bowen finally stopped, she walked over and tried to lift up her son.

'Come,' she said weakly. 'Let's get you to bed.'

Bowen shoved her arm away, sending her stumbling backwards. She regained her balance and slapped Bowen across the face.

Wang Xiao's jaw dropped and hung open, and I found myself feeling sorrier for him than for anyone else in that apartment. I didn't know whether I should take a side, and whose side that should be, or if I should just keep my mouth shut. A familiar feeling came, as if I was invisible again. Even in talks about our family, I wasn't given a place between the two of them. I'd always known that I was on my own, that I existed as

a person separate from others, but to accept that fact –
to walk a solitary path without fear – took a whole
other kind of bravery.

I felt a coldness not on my skin but settling on something inside me. If I hadn't been his wife – if there had
been a clearer line between his life and mine – I might
have been able to understand him better.

I left them there and stuffed as many of my belongings as I could into a small suitcase. Wang Xiao was
gone by the time I dragged my luggage to the door. The
two of them watched me with no intention of saying
anything. In that instant, home felt as though it was
and had always been elsewhere. The apartment was like
a hotel room I'd checked into, with its standard sofa,
TV and coffee table. The only thing that kept me looking back was the piano – *my* piano – planted there on
the floor and unable to leave. How helpless it seemed.

In the car, I remembered the mushrooms under the
sink and debated returning to retrieve them. Although
they hadn't shown any signs of growth, I knew they
were alive under the plastic. I was sure that soon, little
mushrooms would start pushing their way out of the
bag, freeing themselves from the cylinders, growing
upwards and bigger, as though in competition with
each other. I made do with that image and decided that
I'd leave them there.

I turned into Qian Gan Hutong and parked by the

side of the road, making sure that there was plenty of space behind my car so that even a truck would have enough room to drive by. I walked a few steps to the wooden gate. It was heavy when I pushed, but there was something welcoming about it under the dim street light, like a secret entrance waiting for someone to discover it.

Bai Yu wasn't there. No matter how often I knocked and called his name, nobody came to greet me. The door to the house was unlocked, so I finally let myself in. It was dark inside. The light above the piano was turned off too. I checked every room, including the ones he'd never invited me to enter, but there wasn't a single soul. I counted a total of four rooms: the main room facing south, a bedroom, the piano room and the kitchen. Besides the one with the piano, the rest were all rather dirty. Bits of walls had chipped off and fallen. There was mould growing in the corners. If I didn't know better, I'd say that this place had been uninhabited for a long time. I even went out into the courtyard and checked the other buildings on the sides. They were all locked.

Bai Yu must be out somewhere, I thought – I shouldn't panic. But it was late, where could he be? I couldn't imagine him at a restaurant or a bar chatting over a drink and a plate of salted peanuts. Perhaps he'd gone for a walk? I sat on the redwood chair and waited, but I soon became too restless, so I got up to search the rooms again. The closets and cabinets were all empty. The kitchen didn't even have any cooking utensils, only a pile of old newspapers in one of the drawers, a metal bucket and a fire extinguisher by the wall. I leafed through the papers; the latest ones were from 1998. I tried to turn on the gas stove but nothing happened. I remembered that Bai Yu had brewed me some tea the first time I was here, so I dug around for the teapot. I couldn't find it anywhere.

I reminded myself that the place had always looked deserted. Nothing was different. The piano was there. He wouldn't have left without the piano, like I had. There was no foundation to that belief, but it was the only thing I had to hold on to. It felt as though the piano was what gave him form, and without it, he would become a thought, a concept, a blank space. I went outside and walked around the neighbourhood. Besides a few people riding their mopeds home, I didn't see anybody. I arrived at the square where I'd usually find people ballroom dancing, and sure enough, there were some still dancing late into the night. They were dressed in such heavy coats that I couldn't see the contours of their bodies. It didn't appear so much like dancing as figures floating around in the dark. A group of puffy ghosts.

Thinking that Bai Yu could've returned while I was out, I went back to check. The house was as empty as I'd left it. I debated over going to the police and filing a

missing-person report, but quickly realised that I
needed to wait at least twenty-four hours. Plus, they'd
think I was crazy for reporting a man who'd been missing for the past ten years. Out of options, I wrapped
myself up in another coat and waited.

I'd experienced many long nights recently, but never
one as long as this. I couldn't sleep sitting up and I
didn't want to use the bed without his permission. Not
that I would've been able to fall asleep anyway. For
hours, I switched between sitting on the chair like an
honourable statue and rummaging through everything
in the house like a mad thief.

I was beginning to suspect that I really had been
imagining him all this time. Maybe he had died ten
years ago. I looked around for traces of him; an object
or a fingerprint somewhere. There was nothing, only
the piano, but it wasn't like the piano had an engraving
on it that said 'This piano belongs to Bai Yu'. I needed
something more concrete to prove that I wasn't losing
my mind.

Then I remembered the letter he'd sent me months
ago, which gave me a rush of hope, sending me bounc-
ing up from the seat. I dug through my purse and found
it sitting at the very bottom among the other things
that had been in there forever. It was still in the shape
of a paper airplane. I applauded myself for not throwing it out the window that day. I unfolded it and ironed
it out with my hands. I read it a couple of times over,

trying to find a clue of some sort that would lead me to his whereabouts, but all the details seemed insignificant.

There wasn't a phone in the house, let alone a phone book, so there was no way I could tell who Bai Yu had been in contact with besides me. I also couldn't really imagine him picking up the phone and dialling someone's number. I'd always thought that he seemed ancient, tinged with a feeling of being too pure for this world; someone who would never be caught up in daily mundanities such as using a phone.

I pulled out my own cell phone and typed 'Bai Yu' into the search engine. The first article that came up was about his legacy, published two years ago, paired with the news of a man who'd broken Bai Yu's record as the youngest person to win the Tchaikovsky International Music Competition. The article before that one couldn't really be considered news. It was a detailed, day-by-day account of his last few days in the public eye ten years ago. There wasn't much that I didn't know already, so I moved on. Clicking through the pages, most of the headlines were not really about him. His name was only mentioned in lists of famous Chinese pianists.

I cleared the search box and typed in 'Yunnan orange dust'. I expected there to be a lot on this topic, but I could only find two articles. The rest of them were about Yunnan's famous red soil, which the search engine must've decided was what I'd meant. The first article was the one Bowen had shown me, published on 15 November. There wasn't much text – only an image followed by a paragraph:

Since early November, orange dust clouds have been floating in the air in a small town in Chuxiong. The dust resembles pollen. It first settled on the surface of the river. Since then, it has been blown onto the local vegetation and even the houses. In 2014, a river in Zhejiang mysteriously turned red overnight, likely due to illegal dumping. Residents have expressed their concern that the dust might be harmful to their health. The cause in this case is still unknown and authorities are investigating the matter.

The second article was even shorter, as though the writer had forgotten to finish it before it was due and had resorted to submitting the two sentences he'd come up with on the spot:

Unprecedented large plumes of pollen have been observed in the air in Chuxiong. The humidity in the air has also risen, likely leading to an uncomfortable winter ahead.

The photo accompanying this second article had more going for it. Rather than being snapped from above, it showed a close-up view of the town, which made the

orange dust seem more real as well as more alien. The
place really did resemble another planet, like the days
when we had sandstorms in Beijing. It must've been
taken towards the beginning of the spread, since the
roofs of the houses in the distance were still uniformly
grey. There were a few locals in the distance and I wondered whether Julia was among them. I zoomed in but
the photo became too pixelated for me to see any of their
faces. Not that I would've been able to identify her. I held
my face so close to the screen that when my phone
started vibrating, I almost dropped it.

'What on earth happened?' Ruya's voice sounded as
if it was morning already. Every cell in her body was
full of energy.

I could hear Wang Xiao in the background, telling
her to hang up.

'This has got to do with that Julia, right?' she asked.

I couldn't deny it so I stayed silent.

'Come on,' she pushed. 'Talk to me. I feel partially
responsible for this.'

My head began to throb. I could feel my blood invad-
ing my temples. I was afraid that if it kept going, it'd
push a hole through my skin.

'You're not,' I managed to say.

'Where are you?'

'Qian Gan Hutong.'

'Where on earth is that? Do you need somewhere to
stay? You can come stay with us.'

'That's very kind of you. But I'll be fine.'

Hesitantly, she said OK and told me that she was available if I needed any help. After we hung up, I imagined Ruya and Wang Xiao in bed having a chat about the scene we'd caused today. When they grew tired, they'd turn off the lights, go to sleep and dream about things that had nothing to do with me.

NEW GRASS

I waited for a day. Then I waited another day. When I finally couldn't keep my eyes open any more, I collapsed on the floor in the piano room. I was drained, but since I didn't have any food in my stomach, every time I tried to sleep, all I could think about was how hungry I was. I lacked the energy to look for food, so I would close my eyes and try to sleep again. I wrestled with my two biological needs for a few hours until sleepiness finally triumphed and I dozed off on the icy concrete tiles.

I woke up thinking I'd slept until dawn, but it turned out that only twenty minutes had passed. It was eleven in the evening. The nap did a decent job and I felt that my head was clearer, however marginally. I had enough strength to walk to a hole-in-the-wall barbeque restaurant five minutes away. I ordered ten lamb skewers, some chives and a stick of enoki mushrooms. The food looked filthy, like I was about to eat clay from the ground, but the oily, spicy aroma was irresistible. I stuffed all of it down as quickly as possible and called the waitress over to put in another order of vegetables. When I was satisfied, I paid the bill and went back to the courtyard.

When I opened the door, the whole place felt different. It took me a while to identify what seemed off. It was the smell, something that resembled pickled cabbage and damp rice. The odour reminded me of a bathroom cabinet and toiletries that hadn't been aired in a long time. Combined with the food I'd just eaten, it made me want to throw up. I opened all the windows to let in some fresh air, but even by the time the entire house felt like a giant cube of ice, the smell hadn't subsided one bit. Trying to take my mind off the nausea, I decided to play some piano.

In my rush to leave the apartment, I'd forgotten to bring any sheet music with me. I checked inside the bench. It was empty. Not even the sheet music to *Rêverie* was in there, so I resorted to playing from memory. I played everything that came to mind. At times, one melody would dissolve into another. Once, I thought I sensed Bai Yu behind me, but when I turned around, there was only the window that opened up to the deserted courtyard.

That was when I saw the orange mushroom growing out of the door hinge. This time, unlike the two encounters before, I was wide awake. The mushroom ghost wasn't really a single thing any more – there was a cluster – but there was no doubt that what I was seeing was the same. It was brighter. More intense. The mushrooms grew in layers with the larger ones on top, protecting the little ones beneath. I scanned the room and saw that there were a few smaller orange clusters growing in gaps around the room, from the side of the window to the spaces in the bricks. Each one was like a blooming flower.

The stench in the room had become unbearable. I took a deep breath to prevent the food in my stomach from rising up. I wanted to climb out of the window while I could, but my legs were as heavy as steel.

'You won't be able to get out of here,' said one of the orange clusters. I couldn't tell where the voice came from.

'There's a window right there,' I said.

'Then go ahead and try.'

No matter how much energy I tried to summon in my legs, they were stubbornly pinned to the bench. I attempted to push myself up with the help of the piano, but my shoulders felt as if they were holding up a mountain. If I stood up now, I'd throw up everything I'd eaten.

'Why do you want me trapped in here?' I asked.

'I don't have desires like you. It's impossible for me to ...' The mushroom ghost paused, mentally constructing the rest of its sentence. 'To wish for something the way you do.'

It articulated the word 'wish' as though it was in a foreign language. It went on.

'For me, what matters is survival, nothing more. Besides, didn't you come here of your own free will after leaving home?'

I didn't ask how it knew that I'd left home.

'Hey,' it said. 'Can you play that song? The one from last time.'

'Not if you don't let me out.'

'It's beyond my control. All you can do is wait.'

'Wait for what?'

'For someone to open the door.'

I heaved a sigh. I noticed that the clusters were expanding. One that had been the size of a fist was now covering half of the windowpane.

I granted its request and played the nocturne, which took my mind off my situation for a little. The room of mushrooms listened without saying anything.

When I was done, it said, 'That sounded different from last time.'

'Well, last time I was singing it.'

'The instrument is not what I'm talking about. It sounded fresh.'

'Fresh?'

'Like new grass in the spring.'

Though still sluggish, my legs felt like they were able to move now. I carefully got up with the help of my hands and made my way towards the window. The distance couldn't have been more than two metres, but it seemed to take forever. The window was almost entirely covered by orange mushrooms now. It'd only left me a small corner, through which the moon was visible. I couldn't hear a sound from outside. I remembered opening the window to air out the room, but it must've been shut tight now. I used my hands to spread apart the mushrooms, but the layers were endless. The orange light came from under the stems, as though someone was shining a torch from beneath.

Seeing that the door was covered too, and having given up going back to the bench, I slid onto the floor and sat with my back against the only wall that didn't have mushrooms growing out of it. I don't know how long I stayed like that. Gradually, the light above the piano dimmed and turned off, making the orange glow appear brighter, as if it had gobbled up the light.

At some point during the night it had begun to snow again. I felt oddly at ease this time, perhaps because I could see the moon, which was almost a perfect circle. Tomorrow, it'd be bigger, brighter, fuller. It was comforting to know that the outside world was still plodding forward; people would wake from their sleep in a few hours and go about their day. I would be here, away from all of that. I'd left my phone in the main room, so I couldn't even make a call. Not that I wanted to talk to anyone. The mushroom ghost was company enough. I stretched out my legs.

'You told me once that you want to be remembered,' I said. 'Isn't that a desire?'

'You could say that's my only desire. Although, from how I see it, it's not so different from survival.'

'So, survival to you is survival in the memory of others? Are you talking about some sort of a legacy?'

'Legacy only applies when you have something to pass down. I don't. Nothing other than what I am. What do you believe survival to be?'

I reflected on its question; not the part about survival, but the part about belief. What did I believe? There must have been a point in my life when I started doubting, and ever since then, truths have existed on a spectrum, and things I thought were true are perhaps merely beliefs, neither true nor untrue. Do we even need the truth if we have beliefs? Or, rather, do we want the truth? Isn't it the case that despair is often the result of running out of things to believe in, even though truths have always been plentiful? But when has knowing that those truths exist ever given us a sense of peace?

I left the mushroom ghost's question hanging as I contemplated my own and lowered my head to my knees, the same way Bowen was sitting when I saw him last. The humidity was so suffocating that in order to breathe, I had to actively keep my mind on it. If I didn't know better, I wouldn't have guessed it was winter in Beijing. My thoughts began to escape me as I felt as though I was going to faint, but it didn't matter. Even if I fell, the floor would catch me. I allowed a white haze to engulf my mind, as on the day driving to the cemetery, except that this time, it was my choice. I welcomed it.

A tune began to spill into my consciousness. In the beginning, it came like the first droplets of rain. Then it turned into a steady stream. The melody was somewhat recognisable, but I couldn't come up with the name of the piece. Moments later, I realised it wasn't the melody I knew. It was the sound, the way each note was like a silent scream, grabbing on to another in a desperate attempt for cohesion. It was Bai Yu. I was certain of that. I'd listened to his recordings enough that it was easy for me to tell. Had he finally come back? I wanted to see him, touch him, wrap my arms around him. I tried to lift my head, but it was as if I was caught in a foggy swamp, unable to make out which way was north.

As I struggled to regain my senses, the music stopped. Where had he gone? If he was going to leave again, he could at least take me with him, even if it meant that I had to disappear from this world I knew. I wanted to tell him there was nothing that would keep me from leaving here. I activated every muscle and bone in my body and ordered them to move. When I finally managed to sit upright, I looked up and saw the woman in the brown coat standing in front of me. Her lips were a

carmine red this time. With her gloved hands, she
closed the lid of the piano.

There were men talking outside. A layer of winter white
was smeared over everything in the room. The door
was open now and the mushroom ghost was just a tiny
cluster at the bottom of the window. It seemed to have
lost most of its glow. Three young men were walking
around in the main room, discussing something in a
dialect I couldn't understand.

The woman in the brown coat carefully folded the
piano cover into a square. Light spilled onto the velvet,
making it look like there was red glitter sprinkled all
over the fabric.

'Do you have a home?' she turned to me and asked.

For a moment, I had trouble making out what she
was saying. My head felt like it'd been hit by a baseball
bat. As I regained my senses, I remembered that I'd
heard Bai Yu playing the piano. I jumped up from the
floor, which almost sent me falling down again, but
once I steadied my legs I ran into every other room
shouting Bai Yu's name.

All the furniture was gone. There weren't many
pieces to begin with, but now it had all disappeared.
The piano was the only thing that was left.

'Here, take this,' the woman in the brown coat said
to me and handed over a hundred-yuan note. 'You can't
sleep here any more.'

I couldn't say anything. It was as if a cap had been screwed over my windpipe. She must've thought that I'd been squatting in this house. I just shook my head.

She bit her lip and stuffed the note into her coat pocket. The men came into the room and began pointing at the piano. They circled it a few times, bending over to assess it. Then each man grabbed hold of a leg and, on the count of three, started lifting.

'Don't,' I managed to say. 'Don't take it.'

'You're not the owner of this place,' the woman said to me. 'I have to take everything away. You can't keep living here.'

I pressed my hands onto the piano and my weight sent it falling to the ground, almost crushing the foot of one of the men. He yelled something at me.

I coughed a few times, hoping that my voice would come back. It worked.

'You can't take the piano,' I barked back at him. 'You can't take anything. Bai Yu's not back yet.'

The woman's huge eyes got even wider. They were a bright amber, which matched her clothes. Just for a second, she allowed them to shift towards the window, where the orange cluster was glowing weakly. She gave a curious blink before focusing her attention on me again. It was as though the mushroom ghost was nothing stranger than a spiderweb to her.

'Who told you to come?' I asked.

'The owner, of course,' she said.

The men were standing with their hands on their waists, waiting for further instructions. One of them had a cigarette clasped between his lips. The ashes levitated in the air like flakes of silver.

'The owner is away,' I said. 'I'm watching his possessions until he comes back.'

She took a step towards me and reached out her hand, but before touching my arm, she withdrew it.

'I'm sorry to tell you this,' she said. 'But the owner is dead.'

I was flung into a state where language ceased to make sense. None of what came out of her mouth was getting through to me. Her words assaulted me like a swarm of strange insects. In the chaos, each shape came together to form a giant black mass. I couldn't understand what they were or how they'd come to be.

'Bai Yu is dead?' I asked. My voice was far away, as if it had been stripped from my body and heaved into the corner.

Those brilliant eyes of hers stared right into mine for a moment.

'I understand,' she said. 'I'll come back tomorrow.'

I wasn't sure what she understood, but I was certain that I saw, momentarily, behind her poised demeanour and between those words, a hint of grief. It was something that couldn't be concealed by her immaculate outfit and doll-like make-up. At first, she had looked confused, but the longer I studied her face, the more I saw something deep inside betray her. I couldn't say exactly what it was, but it made me think that she, too, felt the weight of the piano bearing down on her.

The woman and the men were gone as suddenly as they'd appeared, leaving me behind to guard Bai Yu's home like an abandoned dog. A frenzy of questions reverberated in my head. I tried to recall the last thing I'd said to Bai Yu. I'd talked about mushrooms, and the thought made me laugh. I had never once really got to know Bai Yu, I realised; my impression of him was nothing more than seeing him as a projection of myself. When it came to the man he really was, I didn't have a clue.

Loss came in all shapes and forms, but it hadn't occurred to me until now that you could lose the things you never had. No matter how much I told myself I'd changed, the truth was that I'd never moved on from being the person who'd failed to listen. I had told myself that Bai Yu needed me, but I had returned here, time after time, for myself alone. I thought about Bowen, the man I wanted to tear open and see inside, and how much of an idiot I'd been to ask for the kind of honesty I couldn't offer myself. Empathy is a liar. It seduces us with the impression of selflessness, yet whatever feelings we think we can fathom are confined by the extent of our own hearts. We are living on our own, in our separate bodies. That was something I didn't know how to accept.

There were people who held themselves as though they were prophets who knew how the next day would unfold. For them, even fear had boundaries that they were aware of. There were others who embraced life's uncertainties and learned to love the imperceptible depths of their fears. They, too, seemed to be at peace. What was I, then, wandering in the middle, terrified of a clear path forward yet equally frightened of the unknown? How could one live a life untouched by such dread?

I took out Bai Yu's letter and read it again and again, until each word seemed as if it was going to evaporate from the page. I read it until it became nothing more than a few scribbles on paper. Like many tokens of memory that cease to retain any emotional meaning if revisited too often, the letter eventually became mundane, like an old grocery list. I folded it up and stored it away.

I kept remembering the mushrooms he'd sent me, as though it'd all happened yesterday. I could see the colours and shapes and feel the textures. The morels looked exactly like tripe. It was written in the encyclopedia I'd bought that morels are good for gut health. Chanterelles have the appearance of yellow morning glories. They smell like apricots. And then there were my favorite ganba mushrooms, a rather uncommon type that tastes like beef jerky. It can only be found in the wild, and only in Yunnan. It grows in layers and looks like a giant pine cone. Because of its rarity and intense flavour, some people call it the king of Yunnan mushrooms.

I also tried to recall Bai Yu's recordings, but these memories felt far away, like the sounds of a waterfall in the distance. I found it difficult to imagine him playing on stage. The Bai Yu I'd known hadn't played a single melody.

All these memories would fade, and when that time came, there'd be nothing left of Bai Yu in my world. If I were completely honest with myself, I'd admit that it didn't make a difference to me whether he was dead or had just disappeared again, in the same way that it hadn't mattered whether he'd been a living person or a shadow. There was nothing wrong with that. We all disappear one way or another eventually.

A dreadful clarity raided my thoughts. It'd been inevitable from the start that a day would come when Bai Yu would be gone. The piano in front of me was going to vanish someday too. It was the truth. We weren't made with endless time between our fingers like noodles we can stretch as much as we see fit. Even the most resilient noodles break at some point. It is the most ordinary and the most profound thing in the world.

I sat down on the piano bench and ran my fingers over the keys. I closed my eyes, hoping one last time that when I opened them again Bai Yu would be standing behind me, but when I did all I saw was the reflection of my two pale hands in the black veneer. Behind the gold Steinway & Sons logo, all the things in the mirrored image were stripped of their colours – even the sun looked cold – and I saw, blurred into a grey dot, the cluster of orange mushrooms by the window.

'Hey,' I said. 'I managed to save the piano. You want to hear me play?'

It didn't respond.

'What about something boring?' I said. 'A plain old fugue maybe?'

Nothing.

'Fine.'

I stood up and spent some time wiping the piano clean with an old T-shirt. Then I took my things and put them into the car boot, bought a stick of candied hawthorn from a lady selling them from a bicycle and roamed the hutongs, sucking on the sweetness. There weren't many people out, especially along the roads without any restaurants. At every intersection, I turned onto the ones that were busier. For as long as I could manage, I didn't want to be alone, even if those brushing against my shoulders were strangers.

I came across a police station and, without a purpose in mind, I walked inside. A female officer at one of the counters looked at me without saying anything before reverting back to her computer screen. What an unpleasant place, I thought. The tiled floors were smeared with muddy water from people walking in with their slush-covered shoes, and the plant in the corner slumped against the wall as if it would rather be dead. I sat on the metal seats and watched the people in uniform working. At one point, the female officer who'd noticed me asked in a kind voice whether there was anything she could do to help. My mouth was busy chewing on a hawthorn so I shook my head.

She gave a sympathetic look and pretended to shiver while saying, 'It sure is cold outside, isn't it?' I nodded and she ended our exchange with a smile.

My phone rang right when I was biting off the last hawthorn on the stick. A Yunnan number popped up on the screen. It must've been Julia. I didn't want to take the call in the police station, so I walked out to answer.

'Is this Yang Bowen?' a man asked on the other end of the line.

I swallowed the hawthorn, which scratched against my throat and made me cough.

'Who is this?' I asked.

'I'm sorry, I must've gotten the wrong number.'

'I'm his wife.'

'Oh, is that so? Are you Li Meilin then?'

I'd never heard of that name before. It didn't take me

long to piece together that it must've been Julia's real
name.

'That's me,' I said without thinking.

He told me that he was a reporter at a small newspaper
that I'd never heard of.

'I wanted to ask your husband whether he'd be willing to give a few words about your son,' he explained.
'Since I have you on the phone, it'd be great, of course, if
you could share a comment too. I'm running an article
on the tragedy of your child's death along with an update
on the phenomenon that's happening in Chuxiong. I
understand that it's a difficult time for your family, so
please allow me to express my condolences. Would you
be able to give an account of what exactly happened the
night your son fell into the river?'

He talked so quickly that I suspected he'd rehearsed
the speech before he called. How did he even get my
number? Was this how reporters were working nowadays? Was he going to plug whatever I was about to say
into his article without some sort of proof that I was the
mother of the dead child? I wondered whether Julia
had been receiving calls like these. When we were on
the phone, she had been so watchful when choosing
her words. Saying them out loud seemed to tug the last
ounces of life out of her. Her voice during our first call
must've been the most defenceless yet unbreakable
sound I'd ever known.

It made me angry to hear this man imply that the

branches of reality could be reduced into a single news article. What maddened me was not so much the belief itself but the fact that this man seemed to have come to terms with it. That was the most unforgivable thing of all.

'Do me a favour and never call again,' I said.

When I hung up, he was saying something along the lines of 'Think of it as a eulogy for your son.'

I searched for Julia's number in my call history and dialled it. I never thought I'd speak to her again, let alone initiate a call myself, but I felt a responsibility to tell her, *don't pick up calls from unknown numbers, because strangers can hurt you too.*

She answered after a few rings.

'I never expected you to call,' she said. 'I'm in Beijing.'

'What do you mean?' I asked.

'I mean, I didn't think you'd have anything to say to me.'

'What do you mean you're in Beijing?'

I heard her tapping on something with her fingers.

'I came here to see Bowen,' she said right before the tapping stopped.

It wasn't rational, but instinctively I stepped behind a jianbing cart and hid myself from the main road. It had always felt as though Julia existed far from my physical reality, and no matter how many times our fates coincided, our bodies would never cross paths. Now, without warning, she'd invaded my space, like an avalanche coming from the south. A current of panic shot upwards to my head. I reassured myself that there was no way we'd run into each other. Even if we did, we would never be able to tell, just as I'd never know if I ran into Boyan at the bus stop.

The old man making jianbing pointed to the hotplate in front of him with a questioning expression, asking me if I wanted one. He looked incredibly old and small. Time must have come along with a hammer and beaten him up. I nodded and held up one finger, to which he gave the most enthusiastic nod before scooping a spoonful of batter onto the hotplate. While he waited for the jianbing to cook, he lit a cigarette and held it in his mouth.

'So,' Julia said. 'Why did you call?'

All of a sudden, I didn't know what to say.

'Do you know about Bowen's sister?' I ended up asking.

'His sister?' I heard Julia opening and closing something. 'He told me about her once. But I don't know much. He just gave an account of the facts.'

'He came home drunk a few days ago,' I said. 'He yelled at his mother.'

'What did he say?'

'He told her that she had no right to talk about grandchildren.'

She said nothing for a moment. I heard her pop open a can of soda.

'The way I see it,' she said, 'he can't expect anyone to understand his pain just by knowing what he's been through. Nobody knows how another person handles pain. That's why we move our lips and tell each other how we feel. If he's pretended all his life that he's come out of the past unscathed, then he can't blame his mother for believing in a strength that he's only pretended to have.'

She took a gulp of the soda and exhaled.

'I know him well,' she continued. 'I'm sure you do too. In a way, he was always like a child to me. I knew his fears and weaknesses. I understood them. But now I realise that I was wrong. The fact of the matter is that he's not a child, and as an adult, fears and weaknesses have consequences if you don't deal with them properly.'

'Is that what you're going to tell him when you see him?' I asked.

She laughed.

'Of course not. None of that has anything to do with me any more. I just want to show him some photos of our son.'

Her laughter faded as the tone of her voice settled into something more sombre, more regretful.

'I do feel sorry for his mother,' she said. 'It's not easy. Being so far away from home. I've been here for a day and I already miss Yunnan. We seem to be particularly attached to the place that birthed us. Yun-Nan. South of the Clouds. It seems like the Cloudy Mountains are always pulling us back, like a yo-yo string.'

The old man brushed the jianbing with plenty of sauce and then sprinkled spring onions over it. He folded it up, bagged it and handed it to me as I stuffed a twenty-yuan bill into his plastic container.

'You know when Bowen came back drunk?' I said into the phone. 'I packed my bags and left home that day. I suppose that, in your words, it was my way of dealing with my fears and weaknesses.'

I glanced at the calendar hanging on the side of the cart. It was flipped to January.

'It's January?' I asked.

'It's the first day of January,' Julia responded.

I hadn't realised that the year had ended and a new one had begun while I was holed up in Bai Yu's house.

'Oh. Happy New Year,' I said.

'Happy New Year.'

That was how the call ended. The oil from the jianbing had seeped through the thin plastic bag and into my palm. I took a bite without thinking and burned the roof of my mouth.

'You better wait a few minutes,' the old man said, laughing. His face was scrunched up like the surface of a straw basket.

I turned around and gave a grateful nod.

'Here's your change,' he said as he tried to hand me some bills.

'Can I use that to buy a cigarette from you?'

He enthusiastically reached into his pocket and handed me the whole pack, along with a white lighter.

'Here, here, take the rest of the pack.'

'It's already January,' I said, taking out a cigarette. 'I didn't even know.'

'You young people are so busy with your lives that you don't even notice the passing of time. When you get to my age, you wake up every morning feeling different.'

'You still look full of energy to me.'

I lit the cigarette and took a drag. It made me light-headed.

He laughed again and shook his head.

'My son's been telling me to go back home for years now. I just want to save up some more money so that I don't need to trouble him when I retire. He tells me that if I get too bored back home, I can always set up another jianbing cart, as a hobby. He knows that I'll get restless if I just sit around. I never really had a passion for making jianbing, but after all these years, I do always find myself out here making jianbing whenever I want to take my mind off something.'

I wondered if everyone has a thing they do; an activity they turn to whenever they feel the need to make sense of things. Everyone should have something like that, I thought.

'He sounds like a caring son,' I said. 'You must be proud of him.'

'Every parent is proud of their child, no matter what they say. Now get yourself somewhere inside before you catch a cold.'

Another customer walked up to the cart, so I waved at the old man and walked away. He gave a smile like that of a wise father sending his child off to live her life, knowing that he wouldn't be able to carry her through every step of the way.

I wasn't even hungry. With the plastic bag hanging on my index finger, I put out the cigarette and continued my aimless stroll. After a few turns, the hutongs ended and opened up to a wider road. Rows of old apartments stood on each side like cargo. One of the windows had a neon sign that read 'Imported Red Wine' in both Chinese and English, with a cell phone number underneath. A block down, there was another with a barber's pole hanging down the top of its window frame. The pole's light wasn't on and I had to walk up to see that the stripes were turning. Did people really decide, upon seeing such signs, to wander into a stranger's home? Were these businesses even legal? I suppose people made all sorts of rash decisions. I'd visited Bai Yu based on a few boxes of mushrooms and a letter.

That autumn evening when I first went to Qian Gan Hutong was beginning to feel as if it'd never happened, like a prophecy that hadn't come true, even as the knowledge of it had already shifted the course of one's life. In that courtyard, Bai Yu had entered my life in the hushed and reserved way that he'd done everything. He had given me something, but took it away before my hands could warm it up. I couldn't even identify what it was I no longer had.

When I walked back to the hutong, the first person I saw was the otter woman. She was in the middle of the street and talking on the phone, her hand scratching an itch on her head. She hadn't spotted me yet, though I doubted she'd remember who I was anyway. Her face was certainly the more memorable out of the two of ours. But if I were to head to my car, I would have to walk past her, and there was no guarantee that she wouldn't give me a hard time again. She might not recall my face but I was sure that she would remember my car. She could even be calling someone to tow it away right now. In a panic, I speeded up and pushed my way into Bai Yu's courtyard before she noticed me.

Behind the gate, the air smelled like boiling vinegar and all the walls were orange.

RECITAL

Every cell in my body was urging me to turn around and flee, hop in my car, lock the doors and drive to the edges of Beijing. To Inner Mongolia. To the end of the world. If I entered the house right now, I might be locked in there forever.

I backed up against the gate and gripped the copper handles in my hands, afraid that they might vanish if I let them go. There was an otherworldly beauty to the bright walls. The more alluring it was, the more terrifying it became. I checked my phone. Discovering that it still had signal, I got an absurd sense of security and even felt encouraged to stay a little longer, as if a few bars on a screen was any indication of freedom.

Having mustered some bravery, I let go of the handles and slowly walked through the second gate and across the courtyard. The door to the main house opened readily when I pushed. The inside of the house was orange too. I stopped my footsteps and stretched my neck inside so that I could see the door to the piano room. It was open, but from where I was, the piano was out of view. Maybe the woman in the brown coat had come and taken it away. I inched a few steps to the left to where I thought the window must've been and spent some time trying to find a hole that would allow me to see inside.

I found none and eventually had to give up. I paced around the courtyard. They hadn't taken away the bicycle, which had, in my mind, become fused together with the walls. When everything else has changed, it is comforting to see those things that have remained in the same place, in the same manner, no matter how the world has flipped and turned.

At last, I walked into the house. The air, wet and stale, attacked my skin and shot right up my nostrils. I wouldn't have been surprised if you'd told me that I'd been thrown into a rainforest in the middle of summer. I took off my coat and glanced at the courtyard one more time before closing the door behind me. Though the walls were glowing orange, the place still felt pitch-black. It shone in a way that didn't cast light on anything but itself, which reminded me of photos I'd seen of coral during the night. The texture of the walls felt the same as the mushroom ghost, as though I had been eaten up by a giant balloon. I imagined the house sucking up all the air, suffocating me. After I died, it'd absorb me too.

Turning left, I saw the piano glowing brighter than

anything else. Apart from the keys, which were still
black and white, the rest of the piano was orange. The
colour was warm and brilliant. I froze at its allure,
which was that of the only instrument standing on
stage after all the guests had left, bathed in a shimmer-
ing light, as if now the performance was finally about to
begin. Taking my time, I walked up and lowered myself
onto the bench. I adjusted the seat to suit my height.

'It seems that she didn't take the piano.' The high-
pitched voice of the mushroom ghost broke the silence.

The room had been awfully quiet up until now and
the sudden noise elevated my heartbeat to an intense
pounding.

'You're a strange person.' This time, I could tell where
the voice was coming from. The source was somewhere inside the piano.

'Hmm?' I said. I realised that I was still holding the
plastic bag with the jianbing inside. I placed it on the
ground.

'You've always wanted to escape this room, but now
you just waltzed in here.'

When my body eased a little, I wiped my hands on
my shirt and ran my fingers over the keys without
pressing down on any of them. I shifted around on the
bench, trying to forget about my damp jeans, which
were glued to my legs.

'I escaped the outside and came in here,' I said. 'If I
were to run away from this place, where would I go?'

'The world isn't divided into the inside and the outside.'

'As I see it, it absolutely is.'

I wondered what time it was in the outside world. Since it was New Year's Day, my father must have been answering the door every few minutes to welcome his guests. My mother had phoned me every year to remind me that I'd need to prepare a piece for my father's New Year's concert, but for the past few, I'd shown up with plenty of gifts and nothing to perform. This year, I hadn't even received her call. She must've finally given up.

'Since neither of us seems to be in a hurry to do something,' I said, 'how about I put on a recital for you? Will you listen?'

'A recital?'

'Yes, a recital. I play. You listen. It's as simple as that.'

'All right.'

It didn't take me long to decide on a programme. I chose the same pieces I'd played for my graduation recital. I did horribly back then, having stopped my practice a few days before the performance to spend my nights drinking and watching films, going to bed as late as I could. Actually, I hardly slept at all. Even when I was so tired that I'd doze off in the cinema, I'd go to the counter when I woke up and buy a large black coffee along with a ticket for the next film.

Throughout my time in university, I spent my summers

taking classes so that I'd graduate early. I must've thought
that finishing my studies ahead of time meant that I had
more talent than others. I had so much energy and determination that it seemed as though I could rocket launch
myself all the way to the planet of fame. But as it turned
out, just like my youth, the fuel I'd been running on would
eventually be depleted.

My final recital was also in the winter. I woke up less
than an hour beforehand and showed up without having warmed up. I remember how sad it was to watch
my fingers struggle to keep up with the notes that they'd
been trained to play for years. They'd clumsily tripped
over the keys, trying to do their work, but the reality
was that they were helplessly ruled by my mind, which,
contrary to what people say, must be weaker than my
body after all. When the body is ill, we take medicine
and we rest. But when the mind is unwell, we believe
we can fix it with sheer willpower; that the decay of the
spirit is less deadly than that of the body. Whoever
decided that the mind is stronger than the body?
Halfway through the second piece, when I couldn't listen to myself any more, I stormed off the stage and
biked back to my dorm as fast as I could.

'The recital will begin in a few minutes,' I announced
to the mushroom ghost. 'By the way, why aren't you a
mushroom any more?'

'I told you, I'm not a mushroom.'

'You sure looked like one.'

There was a layer of condensation over the keys. To my relief, they still felt like piano keys. I used my sweatshirt to dry them off before beginning my warm-up routine. I learned the exercises as a child and have never thought about changing them since. There are a total of five, two of which were taught by my teacher and the rest I copied from my father. My fingers turned out to be so stiff that the exercises weren't enough to loosen them up, so I went on to play some scales. Finally, when I felt as ready as I could be, I wiped the sweat from my forehead, inched my bottom forward to the edge of the bench and straightened my back.

'The first piece is Ballade No. 1 in G minor by Chopin.'

I rested my right foot on the damper pedal and let my eyes close. Pages of music rose to the surface of my mind along with all the pencilled notes in the margins. Unsurprisingly, much of it was a blur. I told myself that even if I were to make mistakes along the way, I wouldn't stop to correct them. No matter what happened, I had to make my way from the beginning to the end. After opening my eyes, I placed my fingers over the keys and allowed their weight to settle just enough so that my elbows could be at ease. The orange surface had no reflections.

The first notes were strong and forceful as they climbed upwards to a pause. On their descent, they fell softly like the night. The orange piano turned out to be

less distracting than I'd imagined. Perhaps it was the slip-
pery and cool surface touching my fingertips and the
timbre of each note brushing against my ear – sensations
that up until now I'd never taken a moment to relish.
They reassured me, energised me, made me miss the
piano like a mother who was waiting for her child to
return from a faraway place. Although I'd spent my life
in the company of this instrument, it was only now that
I was beginning to feel as though I could hear it – hear
myself. The whole world could disappear, I thought,
right then and there, and I wouldn't give a damn.

Little buds of excitement sprouted and flourished
with every bar until a few minutes in, I heard a wrong
note. By the time I'd noticed, I was already a few bars
ahead, but I couldn't remember where I was. My fingers
were racing onwards but my mind came to a blank. I
didn't know what I was playing any more. The music
came to a halt. I panicked. I didn't know where to go
back to. I couldn't remember.

'I'm sorry,' I said. 'I'll start again.'

'You've forgotten how to play,' the mushroom ghost
said.

'I'll remember. I need to make it to the last bar this
time.'

'Things can be forgotten forever at the drop of a hat.
I can only hope that is not the case for you.'

I felt the orange piano glaring at me. I went on to
give the ballade another attempt. This time, I made it

past the point where I'd stopped earlier, but not long afterwards, the same thing happened. I tried again. Again I failed. At some point, the notes in my mind would always become replaced with a white fog. I even performed some mind tricks that I'd learned from a magazine a while ago, but no matter what I did, the notes refused to come back to me. After my fourth attempt, I was beginning to get tripped up before the end of the first page.

'Whatever you're trying to do,' the mushroom ghost said, 'I don't believe it's working.'

That much was obvious. Even my disastrous graduation recital was better. I could only remember fragments of all the pieces I'd learned before. There was nothing strange about forgetting something I hadn't played in years, but what terrified me was the possibility that I'd never be able to learn it again. I'd let all the years of training slip away from me, all the while secure in the belief that if I ever decided, I could easily pick up from where I'd left off.

'Why don't you try another piece,' the mushroom ghost said. Its tone was sombre, without any signs of pity.

The second piece I'd played for my graduation recital was a Beethoven sonata, which was far longer and, as a result, even more impossible to recall. I decided that it wasn't even worth the disappointment, so I started thinking through other options. I could try the Clara

Schumann piece, but I'd only been working on the first
two movements. On top of that, I didn't know it well
enough to play it by heart. While I was flipping through
the glossary of my memory, I remembered *Rêverie*. Of
course! Why hadn't I thought of that? Even though I
hadn't practised it much, I'd been studying the sheet
music first thing in the mornings before my lessons
with Yuyu.

'I have an idea,' I said. 'But you'll have to give me
some time.'

I had to practise. I played through the piece bar by
bar, slowing the tempo down to listen to every note,
particularly the last chord that I'd always got wrong. I
traced the sounds that came from Yuyu's fingers, which
were then replaced by my piano teacher's, and finally
by my father's as he kicked off the concert for his guests.
Each note became clearer than the last. Hours must
have passed. I had no way of telling. Though I was still
having plenty of slip-ups, I was able to play the entire
piece from memory.

'I'm ready,' I announced. 'Let's start this thing over.'

No sounds came from the mushroom ghost, but the
silence was that of a listening audience.

'The only piece on the programme today is *Rêverie*
by Claude Debussy.'

I was beginning to understand why Bai Yu had me
play this piece the first time we'd met. It was a marvel-
lous composition. Listening to it was like watching a

white feather fall from the sky. But I decided I wasn't
going to call upon any images like that. I didn't want to
distract myself. I let my mind rest only on the sounds,
how they came and went, how even the longest ones
were transient, and how beautiful that was.

As I reached for the octave chords, ever so faintly, I
began to feel a pot of anger simmering inside me. At
first, my impulse was to ignore it. I knew this feeling
well. I'd always been able to put a lid over it. Where was
this feeling coming from? It was arguably the most
unfitting emotion for this piece. While I was thinking
this and preparing for the key change, in an instant the
anger boiled and erupted.

All of a sudden, the sensation became new to me and
I didn't have a single idea what to do with it. It was
burning me. The music took on a quality that I hadn't
heard in my own playing before. With every key I
pressed down, the feeling flared up again. I stared into
the orange and it gazed back at me as if trying to pro-
voke me further. Then I figured out what I was angry at.

It was the piano.

Keep playing, I told myself, *you mustn't stop again.* I
knew that if I stopped right now, this anger would
never recede. So I held on to it and allowed it to grow. I
nurtured it with my music. When I reached the last bar,
my throat was dry and I was sweating all over. I wanted
to tear through the walls, run to a park, lie on the
ground and let the icy, wet soil engulf me.

I charged to the kitchen and tugged open the drawer with the old newspapers. Papers in hand, I headed back and stuffed them inside the piano. I made sure to keep them nestled under the strings and touching the wood. Now that the piano was stuffed like a dumpling, I twisted a piece of paper and lit it on fire with the lighter the jianbing vendor had given me. Carefully, I used the tinder to ignite the papers inside the piano. Flames began rising from the instrument. I watched for a while before pressing down on some keys, which had all turned orange. They sounded fine. I added the rest of the papers. Sweat dripped down my neck as the fire heated the room up even more. Moments later, the pulsing flames rose from the inside and climbed up the lid prop to the cover of the piano, burning away its shine and splendour. The orange flames matched the colour of the room perfectly. The instrument looked like it was breathing. I thought it was the most beautiful thing I'd ever seen.

Soon, when the smoke had gathered so much that I couldn't breathe any more, I grabbed the fire extinguisher from the kitchen and tried to remember the training they'd put us through in school. I pulled the pin, aimed it at the inside of the piano and squeezed the handle. My vision became obstructed behind white mist, but I was sure I saw the orange walls fade into a matte grey. After I managed to put the fire out, it looked like snow had made its way inside and settled over the piano. Still finding it hard to breathe, I dropped the fire extinguisher and ran outside.

The sky had turned dark and the street lights were on. The black roofs of houses remained undisturbed, as though they'd been dormant for hundreds of years. I felt heat radiating from my pores and my heart pounding as I turned and ran towards Ditan Park. It must've been earlier than I'd presumed because the park was still open. Thrilled, I bought a ticket, went inside and collapsed onto the ground next to the first tree I came across. I couldn't run any more. The snow leaked through my T-shirt and was freezing against my back. I hadn't even realised that I'd left my coat behind.

All my muscles tensed up from the stinging cold as I stared up at the charcoal clouds overlapping one another. Each of my breaths stretched out a little more. The cold wiped my mind clean and I didn't think about Bowen, Julia, Bai Yu, my parents, my students and the woman in the brown coat. I didn't think about anything, apart from a short moment when the thin silhouette of Nini's co-worker popped into my mind. She faced away from me. Her hands were bandaged and her hair was dyed chestnut. The image didn't linger for long before it dissolved and evaporated with the snow.

I lay there until the security guard came and warned me that the park was closing.

'Aren't you cold?' he asked.

I sat up.

'I should take a hot bath, shouldn't I?' I said.

My back was so numb that I could hardly tell whether it was freezing or burning.

'You better get going then,' he said impatiently. 'The gates are going to close.'

I wanted to tell him that the cold made me feel alive, but he'd already walked away.

BIRTHDAY

When spring came, Julia killed herself.

I had no idea what she looked like, but when I saw the article with the photo of a petite woman in a plain white blouse, an instinctual certainty settled in my stomach, and I knew it was her.

I was drinking iced oolong next to an open window and doing my routine afternoon search for updates on the orange dust. For the past few months, I'd been keeping up with the story. I say that, but there really hadn't been many relevant reports at all. Most days when I typed 'Yunnan orange dust' into the search bar, there was nothing new. I had only found two more articles about it since the first ones I'd seen. They were written by the same journalists, both reporting that sometime in the middle of winter, all the orange dust had landed on something and there was no more in the air. They speculated that it was because of the seasonal change. Despite the fact that winters in Yunnan were usually quite mild, this past one had been particularly cold.

Apparently, Julia had hanged herself with a shower curtain in the middle of the night. She'd done it from one of the trees by the river. She must've taken a shower beforehand because when they found her, her hair had frozen through.

'From afar she looked like a large icicle,' a witness said. 'I didn't think she was real.'

'I thought she was a ghost,' another added.

They'd only blurred out her eyes, so I could see how thin she'd been. The shape of her face was like a shrivelled strawberry. The photo they'd chosen had her facing the camera in front of a blue background. She was pursing her lips so tightly that I could imagine blood flowing down her chin and staining her white blouse the moment after the photo had been taken. The image frightened me, so I downed my iced tea and began pacing around. Behind the pixelation, I could sense Julia's eyes looking right at the camera – at me. Maybe they were kind eyes, but I couldn't tell, and all the different possibilities made me uneasy. To clear my head, I thought I'd get dressed and go shopping for a piano.

I'd moved into a small apartment near Beixinqiao back in January, and ever since then, I'd been wanting to buy a piano. The only reason I hadn't managed yet was because Bowen had offered to transfer my old one over, but twice now, I'd cancelled our appointment with the moving company out of fear of going back to that apartment to face him and my mother-in-law.

I threw on a coat over my pyjama shirt and hopped into a pair of jeans. If I could get ready with such little effort every day, just how much time had I wasted getting dressed all these years? Outside the compound gates, I turned north. It was a splendid day – one of those April afternoons when you can feel the abundance of oxygen in the air. Ever since the weather had warmed up, I'd pretty much stopped driving and had been riding the subway more frequently. I'd once despised the rotten smell that permeated the subway cars – a stench that was sometimes mixed with the scent of disinfectant and other times with dirt, and always made me want to throw up. But recently I had begun to enjoy the rides. I liked looking at the faces. No matter what emotions they showed the world, they were indifferent to me. That made me feel less alone.

I paused my footsteps as I passed the gate of Yonghe Temple. I hadn't been inside in years. Most of it was hidden behind the high walls, so that all I could see from where I stood were two layers of mustard-coloured roofs. Thinking that I should burn some incense for Julia, I bought a ticket and went inside.

From the entrance gate, I could see puffs of smoke rising from the incense burners, obscuring the red structure behind. It was almost closing time, so there wasn't a queue at the incense booth. In a few minutes I was standing in front of the main hall, holding three sticks of incense to the burner flame. I did what I thought was correct – I closed my eyes, held the sticks to my forehead and bowed three times. I wanted to say something to Julia, but I couldn't think of anything, so I ended up whispering, 'I'm sorry.'

When I was finished, I saw a middle-aged American woman looking at me and mirroring my movements. I didn't know why I thought she was American; it must've been because she resembled the actress in *Groundhog Day*, who I assumed was American. She smiled at me. I wanted to tell her that I didn't really have any idea what I was doing. She should've followed the woman to her left who was kneeling on the stone ground and pressing her palms together in front of her chest. She looked much more like a devoted believer. Better yet, she could've asked a monk. I gave my best attempt at a smile back before walking away.

As I visited each of the halls, I prayed for Julia and then for Bai Yu. Now that I thought about it, they'd both talked in such a way that every sentence sounded like it could have been their last. They were kites tied to this world by a string. Now that the string was cut, I prayed that they'd be free, wherever they were. Whether it was my imagination or not, I really felt as if the statues were listening.

On my way out of the temple, I received a call.

'Are you home?'

It was Bowen.

'I'm at Yonghe Temple,' I said.

'I'm in front of your building.'

'I didn't know you were coming.'

'Do you have other plans?' he asked.

'Not at all. I was about to come home now.'

I couldn't tell him that I'd been planning to go shopping for a piano since he still believed I intended to take my old one. There was also no chance I was going to say that I was praying for Julia, whom I believed was dead. He would question how I knew and I wouldn't have been able to answer. I couldn't have said, 'It's just a feeling I had when I saw the photo. A strong feeling that makes me certain.' Bowen didn't think that way.

He was waiting in the car when I got back. He rolled the window down and called to me as I passed by. Although we'd been in touch, this was the first time we'd seen each other since the day I'd left him sitting by the shoe cabinet with a stomach full of alcohol and anger. Today, his eyes were smiling.

'Happy birthday,' he said. 'Let's go get duck. I've found us a place.'

It was our tradition. Every year, for my birthday, we'd get Peking duck at a restaurant that neither of us had been to. It'd begun in the first year we started dating, when he asked me what my favourite food was.

'Peking duck,' I'd responded without thinking.

He'd teased me and said, 'That's not so original. I was expecting something more musician-like.'

'And what would that be?'

'Something French maybe.'

'Something French?'

'Aren't all those composers French? Like Chopin?'

When we met, Bowen had no interest in classical music, but the few times I'd gone on about some composer or a piece I'd been teaching, he was always keen to listen. Then a couple of hours later, he would've forgotten most of the things I'd told him. I knew that he wasn't pretending to care; he really did want to learn more, but his mind was always filled with other matters. It was out of his control.

'Chopin was born and raised in Poland,' was all I'd said.

'What's Polish food then?'

'I have no idea. Maybe we can go to Poland someday and find out.'

He'd laughed. 'I'd rather go to France first. All right, let's go to Dadong for duck, then.'

'I want to go to a restaurant I haven't been to before.'

'What if it's not good?'

'Then we'll know never to go again.'

That was how the tradition began. At the beginning, the restaurants we went to were subpar at best, but the enjoyment was in discovering them. To be honest, we didn't care much about the duck at all. Later, we found ourselves going back to the same few places as our attention turned more towards the food and away from each other. My birthday began to feel like just another day in our lives.

I told Bowen that I was wearing my pyjamas underneath, so I needed to change first.

'Come upstairs,' I said. 'It's only five o'clock.'

He hadn't seen my new apartment yet, but he didn't care to look around and just perched against the window, as if whatever was going on outside was more deserving of his attention. I was OK with that. There was not much to show anyway, only some cheap furniture and a pair of speakers. I poured some oolong tea into a mug for him.

He always lost weight during spring and this year was no exception. His pants were loose and the waistband scrunched together under his belt. Every time he moved, his tucked shirt would rise up a little.

'What were you doing at Yonghe Temple?' he asked as I handed over the mug.

'Just praying,' I said.

'My mother was there a few days ago,' he said. 'Funny that you both had the same idea.'

'How is she doing?'

'We don't talk much,' he said. 'She sleeps a lot.'

I tried to come up with something to say.

'Well, I'm sure she's glad that winter is over,' I eventually said. 'I imagine she's not used to northern winters at all. Though I heard that this year,' I added, 'it was particularly cold in Yunnan too.'

He drank all the tea in one go and looked at his watch.

'Aren't you hungry?' he asked. 'I didn't have lunch. I'm starving. Go get ready. I'll wait here.'

I changed into a silk dress and a beige cardigan and quickly smeared some concealer over my dark circles. In the mirror, my face was that of a woman without love. There wasn't anything wrong with it, only that it lacked a kind of shine – something that resembled a warm light being switched on under the skin. No amount of make-up would help. I left it at that. Piling on more would only make me look worse.

It was a Friday afternoon and the traffic was horrendous. Bowen drove as if he'd been blessed by the angel of patience. He would wait for the car in front of us to move twice before letting go of the brake. At first, the taxi driver behind us would honk at us to inch forward at every opportunity, but soon he must've realised that Bowen was not going to do things his way.

'I usually take the subway now,' I said. 'It's faster.'

Bowen rolled his window down.

'When I came to Beijing,' he said while lighting a cigarette, 'there were only three lines on the subway. I lived in the suburbs. To get to work, I had to take a bus and then two trains. It was then that I knew I wanted to work for a car company.'

'Seriously? You never told me that before.'

He looked at me and smirked. 'No, but I did swear to myself that I was going to buy a car within the next two years.'

'Did it happen?'

'Not even close. Turned out it was much harder and more expensive than I'd thought.'

He took a drag on his cigarette and then dangled his arm out of the window.

'I realised that compared to buying a car,' he said, 'it was easier to move into the city.'

We chatted about all the brands of electric cars that had started showing up on the streets in the past few years, until we swerved off the Third Ring Road. As we pulled up at the restaurant, Bowen told me to get a table first while he looked for parking.

It was a beautiful restaurant that looked like all other beautiful restaurants. The tables were set with crisp white tablecloths and positioned rather far from one another, and the part of the kitchen where the ducks were being roasted was visible behind a large glass pane. After I had waited for a bit, Bowen joined me and we were shown to a round table towards the back.

The evening was pleasant enough. We had a duck and two other dishes along with a bottle of red wine. Neither of us mentioned the events that had taken place on the night I'd left, but unlike before, he wasn't trying to avoid anything. I recognised this when I asked how Wang Xiao was doing, explaining that I hadn't

seen him in months. I'd expected Bowen to change the
subject to avoid talking about that night, but he
answered my question without any hesitation. I was so
surprised, I didn't actually comprehend what he was
saying at all. It made me think that if I did decide to ask
about that night, he'd be just as forthright and sincere
in his response.

But I chose not to. If tonight was my only chance to
get some answers out of him, then I'd missed it.
Unexpectedly, I felt at ease with that. There must've
been a moment when all the questions in my mind had
unravelled and disappeared. Now I had brushed so
closely against the answers I'd thought I wanted, I'd
come to understand that those emotions that once bru-
tally overwhelmed me had drifted away. Perhaps many
such moments of letting go come like that – quietly and
unremarkably. There were no answers that I needed
from him any more.

We'd both had some wine, so we called a driver to
take us back. It was a young man who arrived on a
small electric bike that he folded and stored carefully
in the trunk. He put on some white gloves and started
the car. After we told him the address, for the rest of
the ride none of us said another word. When the car
dropped me off at my compound, Bowen told the
driver to wait as he stepped out to say goodnight. His
face was flushed – he'd never been able to handle wine
very well. His shirt was untucked now, which made it

obvious that he'd lost even more weight than I'd thought. It dawned on me that as winter had turned into spring, time had passed for him too. My understanding of him had halted the night I'd left him with his emotional instabilities strewn across the floor and his phone thrown at his mother's door. How could I know how many of those shattered pieces he'd picked up since then?

I told him that if he didn't want to go home, he could stay at mine. We were married, after all. He seemed happy with my offer and strode back to the car to let the driver know. The driver parked the car, returned the keys to us and rode away on his electric bike.

Bowen seemed exhausted. He walked past the living room and went straight for the bed.

'Change into this,' I said as I dug out a large T-shirt from the closet and handed it to him. 'I'm going to brush my teeth. There are cups in the kitchen if you want water.'

When I came back, he was already asleep. I turned off the light and got under the covers too. Side by side, we lay on a bed that was familiar to me but new to us. I turned my head to face him. I hadn't drawn the curtains and the white evening light desaturated his skin, which, together with his bony face, made him look like a corpse. My body froze in fear. I stayed like that for a few minutes until his breathing deepened, giving him back his life. Relieved, I rolled over to the other side

and checked the clock. It was past midnight. I was a
year older.

I woke up at five in the morning, and Bowen was crying
in the bathroom. At first, I was so disoriented that I
thought someone had broken into the apartment. Then
I remembered that Bowen had slept here. When I
opened the bathroom door, he was sitting on the toilet
in his underwear and the T-shirt I'd given him. His
hands clenched his hair, keeping his head from falling
downwards. I'd never seen him cry before. His back
trembled as he tried to suppress the choking sounds he
was making, but the more he struggled to hold them in,
the louder they were when they burst out of him. I
could only stand there and watch.

His weeping came in waves. Whenever I thought
he'd stopped, it would start again, as though he was
trying to drain out all that was left of him and begin a
new life. When it finally stopped, he blew his nose with
some toilet paper and stared at the line of patterned
tiles running across the bathroom walls.

'I had a son,' he said, sitting hunched over on the
toilet.

'I know.' My voice came out brittle and weak, so I
cleared my throat and repeated it.

'He's dead now,' he said. 'His mother is dead too.'

'I know.'

He took a deep breath.

'I also have a sister. To be honest, I don't remember much of the days we spent together. I don't remember her voice. I don't remember what we did together. I've always told myself that at least I remember what she looked like, but every day, I feel like I'm forgetting her face a little more.'

He paused to wipe his nose.

'Even if I manage to etch her face into my memory,' he continued, 'it tears me apart to think that if I see her now, I won't recognise her. She may as well be dead to me.'

He turned towards me. He looked like a different man.

'You already know all of this, but I wanted to tell you myself. I want to apologise.'

I walked up to him and held his head to my abdomen.

'I don't know what to do,' he said.

'Come,' I said, taking the toilet paper from his hand. 'Let's go lie down.'

In bed, neither of us said anything. We had spoken enough. We lay under the duvet, his hand resting over mine, and together we waited for the sun to rise. Gradually, when the morning light shone through the window and onto the wooden floor, we got up and prepared for the day.

ANISE

A few days later, on Guanghua Road, I walked by the woman in the brown coat, though she was wearing a black cardigan now. Underneath, she had on a pair of white pants and beige ballet flats. Her long hair was tied into a low ponytail. I was on my way to Yuyu's when I spotted her waiting in line for an ATM. From the way she stood, I recognised her even from the back. She was like a mannequin – her feet neatly placed parallel to one another; her arms hanging down the sides of her body; her back as straight as a ruler.

When she moved away from the ATM, I called out to her. I had questions for her and coincidences like this didn't happen every day. This could very well be the last time I saw her. When she had shown up at the courtyard, I hadn't been able to say anything. Today, I was composed, determined, and above all else, I missed Bai Yu. It wasn't the kind of feeling that smothered the body and clogged up the mind – I'd managed to go on with my days as usual. But at the end of these days, his absence in my life left me going to sleep a little lonelier than before.

Trying to remember who I was, the woman stared at me with her deer-like eyes.

'We met at Qian Gan Hutong,' I explained. 'At Bai Yu's place. You came to take away the furniture.'

She nodded her head cautiously, plainly still confused as to what I wanted.

'I would like to talk with you,' I said. 'Do you have a moment?'

With the same alarmed expression, she tried her best to give a polite smile.

'There's a coffee shop nearby,' she said. 'We can go there.'

She walked in an unhurried manner and I slowed my footsteps to keep pace with her. She moved her bag to the other side so that it wouldn't bump into me. We passed a few embassies with flags I didn't recognise. All the while, she looked forward as though she was alone. On occasion, I'd get a waft of her perfume. It smelled like anise.

I checked my watch. I was already twenty minutes late to my lesson. Seeing that the woman wasn't going to say anything until we arrived at the coffee shop, I figured I'd use the time to give Yuyu's mother a call. In the background, I could hear her newborn baby crying. I explained that I'd had something urgent come up, so we agreed that we'd reschedule the lesson to another day. She and I had grown closer these past few months. When she heard that I'd moved into a new place by myself, she started inviting me over for dinner. Sometimes, we'd go out to eat and she'd bring Yuyu along. We always had hotpot. It was Yuyu's favourite. She'd also introduced me to a few of her friends who needed piano teachers for their children.

The woman stopped in front of a coffee shop on Jinbao Street. She went in first and held the door open for me. It was dark inside; the windows did not let in much light. Every chair was different but all were wooden, antiquated. We each ordered a cappuccino at the counter. I offered to pay, but the woman beat me to it by handing over a hundred-yuan note that had already been in her hand. It came out of nowhere and reminded me of the time she had tried to give me money. We sat down at a large table next to the window. The leather on the sofa was cracked all over.

'I want to know more about the courtyard at Qian Gan Hutong,' I said.

She nodded. Up close, those brilliant eyes of hers outshone her other features and dominated her entire face.

'Do you know the owner?' I asked.

'I lived there when I was young,' she said. 'The owner is long gone.'

'But the place wasn't empty. Someone lived there. I knew him.'

Her eyebrows furrowed in thought.

'It was a man named Bai Yu,' I said. 'The famous pianist . . .'

'I first met Bai Yu when I was a child,' she said. 'I lived in the courtyard with my family.'

The barista bearing our cappuccinos interrupted the conversation. The woman looked up and nodded as an expression of gratitude. When we were left alone again, she cupped the drink between her hands and rotated it absent-mindedly.

'Was it you who burned the piano?' she asked.

Her question caught me by surprise.

'I'm sorry,' I said quickly.

'You know, when I went back and saw the piano all scorched and wrecked, I felt a sense of relief. My first thought was, why didn't I think of doing that?'

She leaned back and nestled into her seat.

'Ten years ago,' she continued, 'before Bai Yu disappeared, he came to me and told me he felt like he'd already died. He said that with everything he'd done, he still hadn't managed to find any meaning in the piano; anything that could validate his existence.'

She shifted again in her sofa, crossing her legs and then uncrossing them again.

'I'd never seen him like that,' she said. 'He had this look, like there was no one else in the world besides him. It frightened me. I stayed with him all night, but he didn't say a single word. The next day, he was gone.'

I recognised something in her; something that crippled me, too, on days when the sky was cloudy and the air was heavy. It was the weary look of a woman beyond heartbreak, where pain didn't sting any longer but rather pulled her down with an authority and inescapability akin to gravity.

I let her continue.

'After he disappeared, I realised that even though we'd known each other for over twenty years, he'd hidden a big part of himself from me.'

She shook her head, changing her mind.

'No, he didn't hide anything. In fact, it was the exact opposite. He tried hard to show me what he lived for, and I tried equally hard to see. But the more we tried, the more we failed, until neither of us had the energy to keep going any more. He believed that what he needed could only be found in the piano. A cold and dead instrument that can't play itself was not going to be the answer. He just couldn't see that.'

One of her hands dropped a sugar cube into her cappuccino while the other stirred with a spoon.

'The night he came to me, I made up my mind. I decided that I'd stick with him while he searched for what he needed, no matter how many years it was going to take, even if it meant a lifetime. He was sealed like an envelope that wasn't addressed to me, but I would hold him through it all anyway. I even told him that. But now I know how irresponsible that thought was. I was never going to be able to do that.'

She gave a strained smile.

'Turns out it's possible to be deeply in love with a person you don't know,' she said. 'When one is in love, one always begins by deceiving one's self and always ends by deceiving others. Oscar Wilde wrote that.'

Still smiling, she said, 'You remind me a little of Bai Yu. Especially the time you threw yourself at the piano and insisted that we leave it there. Although I have to say, I didn't expect you to burn it down. You could've set the whole house on fire, you know? You're brave to have called out to me. What if I reported you to the police?'

She chuckled. What an impeccable face, I thought, so much so that it took on an artificial quality.

'Let me ask you something,' she said. 'Is he gone? For good?'

'The day you came with the men, I was waiting for him, but he never came back.'

'His family officially declared him deceased a few days before I came to take away the furniture. They'd given up hope long ago, but I never did. I'd managed to convince them to wait a few more years, but his parents are old now and they needed something definitive. I understand that. Not many people are as stubborn and unable to let go as I am.'

'Aren't you going to ask me about him?'

'Believe me, I want to grab your shoulders and shake all the information out of you. I want to know how he was doing, if he'd put on some weight at last, if he'd also felt himself getting older every day. It's been ten years and finally I have somebody to ask. All the questions I've held inside me could blow my heart into pieces.'

She paused and took a deep breath.

'But it's best for me to believe that he's dead,' she said, and laughed at herself. She turned to look out at the street. 'I never imagined I'd say this, but I feel better this way.'

I joined her in observing the people outside. My eyes came to rest on two women sitting in an Audi parked in front of the coffee shop. One of them was adjusting her earring.

'What if he comes back again?' I asked.

'Do you think he will?'

'I don't know. He did before.'

'If he does, I'll cook him a nice meal.'

She drank from her cup.

'I cleared out the courtyard,' she said. 'If you want to go take a final look, you should do that soon. Bai Yu's family is doing some renovations right now. They're going to break it up and sell it as three separate units.'

Hearing her talk about the courtyard, I remembered something.

'When you lived in the courtyard, did you ever see the walls turn orange?' I asked.

She took another sip of her drink and licked the foam off her upper lip. She dabbed at her mouth with a napkin as she meditated on how to respond.

'No,' she said. 'I never saw that.'

We talked for a while. She had a way of talking that I found incredibly captivating. Every sentence ended exactly where it needed to. Although she did most of the talking, she didn't come across as a chatty person; she didn't even appear as if she wanted to speak. It made me think that if you told her that she could never say anything again, she'd be all right with it. Maybe with those expressive eyes of hers, she didn't really need a voice.

She told me that when she was a child, before the buildings in the courtyard were consolidated, they'd been three separate units. Bai Yu's grandmother lived in the main building and her own family lived in the other two. It wasn't uncommon for those who shared the same courtyard to grow close and resemble one big family. She and Bai Yu first met when he spent a summer there. After the woman's family moved out, Bai Yu's grandmother lived alone for some time before she passed away. The next time the woman saw Bai Yu again was when they started the same high school. He had already become a little famous by then.

During the time they were apart, Bai Yu had changed. He didn't care for friends or school and spent all his free time with the piano. His parents had to force him to go to sleep at night. Other people admired his dedication, but the truth, according to her, was that he could see no other choice. He put up a friendly façade, but it was clear that he cared more about the piano than about other people. She became his closest and only friend. They listened to music together and he talked to her about the piano. She was the one person he could be sincere with, but oftentimes, he'd withdraw himself even from her.

'There wasn't any joy in it for him,' the woman told me. 'When we wake up, we hardly ever consciously acknowledge the pleasure of being able to live another day, do we? For him, being with the piano was like waking up. He never stopped for a moment to enjoy it.'

'You say you don't understand him, but it seems that you know him better than anyone else.'

She laughed. 'He's a prodigy, isn't he? How could I understand the workings of a prodigy's mind?'

Then, with a more serious expression, she continued.

'Then again, shouldn't we all be chasing after something? Pursuing whatever it is with all we've got? I'm starting to think that, in a way, he was more normal than anyone else.'

Right as she finished her sentence, we heard thunder in the distance. The coffee shop was so dark I hadn't noticed the sky turning black. It was only four in the afternoon, but it looked like the middle of the night. A storm was brewing towards the west.

'I'd better get going,' she said. She raised her cup in the air, for a toast. 'To all music lovers.'

We clinked our cups together. She finished her drink and I pulled the table towards me so she could get out. The scent of anise drifted my way as she squeezed by. Outside the window, she waved goodbye but turned away before I could wave back.

Just like that, she was gone. I had the feeling that I'd just woken up from a dream. If it wasn't for the lipstick mark she'd left on her cup, I'd question whether our conversation had really happened. We didn't even ask for each other's names. It hardly made a difference anyway; we both knew that if we saw each other again, we wouldn't exchange any words. Maybe we'd smile at each other, maybe we wouldn't, but words were unnecessary from here on.

I finished my now cold drink, and called for a taxi.

STORM

The taxi drove towards the flashes in the sky and arrived at the corner of Qian Gan Hutong. I paid and got out of the car, attacked by a gush of chill wind. I hastened my footsteps.

When I approached the gate of the courtyard, a group of construction workers were on their way out.

'Can I go inside for a minute?' I asked the one who was carrying a ladder on his shoulder.

He turned slowly and gave me a look that told me he didn't give a damn. I decided to forget about asking for permission and let myself in as usual. Most of the workers were gone, except for a young man in the main building who was busy skim-coating the walls. The buildings on the sides were sealed off behind plastic sheeting. I looked around for the bike, but they must've taken it away.

The young man gave me a cold look before returning to his work. The air tasted like paint. A half-finished bottle of water sat atop planks of wood that were piled up in the corner. The place was naked. Patches of grey could be seen on the otherwise white walls, the floor was all concrete, cigarette butts were everywhere and the wooden ceilings were exposed. It felt like I was coming here for the first time. I didn't know what I'd expected, but my immediate sense of detachment came as a surprise. It was hard to imagine that music had been played in this brick box. I looked around for the orange mushroom. I went to every room and checked all the corners, but I couldn't find even a trace of it ever having been there. Back in the piano room, I leaned my back against the window and looked at the centre of the room where the piano used to be. The warm ceiling light was just an open cable now; I tried to imagine myself sitting on the bench and Bai Yu bent over behind me.

It was then, staring at an empty room stripped of remnants of the past, that I realised I loved Bai Yu. It wasn't romantic love. It wasn't as complicated. He made me see the simple fact that we are not tied down to this world; we are in pursuit of it. That is how I loved him.

A thought came to me. *I could buy this place!* I entertained that idea for no longer than a few seconds before admitting there was no way I could afford it. Even though the woman had told me that they were selling the courtyard as three smaller units, I still didn't have enough money for even this part of it.

My phone vibrated in my purse. Bowen's name was on the screen.

'I was hoping you'd help me out with something,' he said. 'Ma is sick. She's staying at Chaoyang Hospital right now.'

'What's the matter?'

'It's her blood pressure. It's not too serious, but it took a lot of trouble finding her a bed at the hospital, so I told her to take this opportunity to have a full body check-up.'

'Do you need me to take care of her?'

'I found her a caretaker, but the thing is . . .' He spoke hesitantly. 'I've just moved to Shanghai.'

I waited for him to elaborate.

'For work,' he added.

'For how long?' I asked.

'I don't know,' he said. 'At least until autumn. So I need someone to make sure she's OK.'

'Sure. Send me her room number. I'll head over there now.'

'I appreciate it,' he said. 'I really couldn't say no to this trip. I gave it a lot of thought—'

'I understand. Best of luck.'

He must've wanted to say something else; I heard him take a breath in. He held it there and eventually let out a sigh.

'Thank you,' he said. 'How are you doing?'

'Couldn't be better.'

*

The storm began on my way out of the courtyard. It rained with so much force there wasn't even a rhythm to the raindrops. The trees that lined the streets swayed in the wind as though they were underwater. It took me a good ten minutes to find a taxi and in the meantime I became drenched. Shivering, I asked the driver to turn off the air conditioning in the car, after which he gave a proud laugh and warned me to check the weather forecast in the future.

'Even I brought an umbrella with me,' he said. 'All I do is drive in a car all day, but every night, I still make sure to watch the weather forecast. I'm always prepared like that, in all aspects of life. You see what I'm saying, young lady? It's not about the weather, it's about the attitude!'

'You're absolutely right.'

Outside the window, all the tail lights blurred into little red moons in the dark.

I went home first. To avoid catching a cold, I took a quick shower, got changed and slurped down some hot water. Fully prepared this time with a raincoat and an umbrella, I braved the storm again. When I arrived at the hospital, the reception area was swarming with people. The lifts were moving slowly, so I walked up the stairs, passing by all sorts of patients. Only one of them could stand up straight without any sort of support.

I asked a nurse for directions to my mother-in-law's room. When I went inside, she was lying on the bed

next to the window, watching the muted TV that was
mounted on the wall. The air smelled like disinfectant,
iodine, damp blankets and unbrushed teeth. It was as
though the entire room was decomposing. The other
bed was taken by a younger woman who was so skinny,
I could see the shape of her skeleton. In a flash, I felt
sick, as if all the minor discomforts in my body came
together and formed a large tumour.

Seeing my mother-in-law's face didn't make me feel
any better; she looked like she'd aged ten years. She
saw me and lifted her head. Her lips were dry and stuck
together when she talked.

'Did Bowen come with you?' she asked.

'He's at work.' I sat on a chair next to her bed and
poured her a glass of water from her thermal bottle.
'How are you feeling?'

'Oh, you know. I'm just light-headed all the time.'

'Bowen told me he hired you a caretaker.'

'He did,' she said, wriggling under the blanket as she
tried to sit upright. I reached over and helped her. 'I
told her to go. I didn't want to spend money on an
unnecessary caretaker. I can do everything myself.'

She sighed. Long inhale. Short exhale.

'Bowen asked you to come, didn't he?'

I nodded.

'He didn't come home the other night,' she said. 'He
told me he was with you.'

'He was.'

'I'm glad to hear that.'

After a brief silence, I said, 'Unfortunately, I'm not pregnant.'

I wasn't sure why I'd said that. I tried my best to save the awkward moment by forcing out a playful laugh that ended up sounding more like a sneeze. I was about to change the subject when my mother-in-law reached out and cradled my hand in hers.

'I'm sorry,' she said with a vulnerability that was ill-suited for such a black and stormy day. It made me think that even the rain could kill her.

She patted my hand and said, 'You look tired.'

I was reminded of my mother. Growing up, my immune system had been as fragile as an orchid. Whenever I came down with a cold, I'd pretend to be healthy so she wouldn't worry. 'You look tired,' my mother would say all the same. She'd set a glass of water on the nightstand and put me to bed. When I woke up, there'd always be medication and a bowl of wontons waiting on the table.

'After I'm done here,' my mother-in-law said, 'I'll be moving back to Yunnan.'

She paused.

'You should move back home too,' she added.

I almost told her about the town that had become covered in orange dust, but thought better of it as her eyes met mine. It seemed that, in a formless but unquestionable way, she already knew. Even though she might not have been informed of the events, there was an understanding that things were different now back home. Neither of us could return to the same place we'd left behind.

'I'm going to get you some clothes from the apartment,' I said, standing up. 'Do you need anything else?'

'Can you bring me a pen and some paper? I want to write a letter to Bowen. You don't need to come back tonight. I'll be fine.'

'Of course.'

On my way out, she said, 'I missed listening to you play the piano. It's been so quiet.'

I smiled and left the door open behind me to let in some air.

At the apartment, I packed some clothes and supplies for my mother-in-law into a duffel bag. Four of Bowen's blue shirts hung loosely on the racks in the closet. He'd taken all the white ones with him. It was chilly, so I turned on the heater, took another hot shower and climbed into bed. The duvet carried Bowen's scent as I pulled it over me. It didn't call to mind the years I'd spent with him in this particular bed, but rather it reminded me of my birthday when, lying side by side, we'd held hands and listened to the gentle breathing of the dawning sky.

Tonight, the sky was another story. Thunder roared and the wind responded by whistling through the trees.

It felt as though the building was being rocked left and right and could snap anytime and send me plummeting into the earth. It was too loud to go to sleep, so I went to the bathroom and opened the basin cabinet.

Inside, there were hundreds of bright orange mushrooms glowing in the dark. They'd burst through the plastic and grew upwards in layered clusters, like those I'd seen in the courtyard. The species towards the inside of the cabinet had caps that were flat and wide. All the other ones were smaller and rounder. Together, they looked like a swarm of jellyfish floating through the night.

'Hello?' I said.

There was no response.

I kneeled on the floor and reached for one of the smaller ones. The air in the cabinet was cold, like I'd opened a fridge. I twisted the stem around until the mushroom loosened and detached from the substrate. Sitting between my fingers, it glimmered like a light bulb. Droplets of water balanced on its cap, as though it was protected by a layer of membrane. I took a deep breath in. I smelled the earth; it was like lying in the woods on a spring morning and seeing just how much life there is in this world. The wind outside grew louder. As I cradled the little thing in my palm, my heart drummed a steady beat.

BICYCLE

The boy on the red bicycle rings his bell at every person in his way. It is the last day of school before the New Year. It's a few minutes past four in the afternoon and he is scheduled to be at his piano lesson, but when he was let out of school, he went headlong in the opposite direction. He shifts his weight between the pedals, each of his hurried breaths visible in the wintry air.

Bai Yu is heading towards his grandmother's home. When he arrives, he doesn't check to make sure he's at the right address as he lifts his left leg to the right and jumps off his bike before it even comes to a stop. In a rush, he stuffs the padlock into the back wheel, hoping that anyone who considers stealing it will be fooled into thinking that it's locked. There is a box of mushrooms sitting next to one of the stone lion dogs. He smiles. He picks up the box and storms past the wooden gate. He almost trips over the door sill but he doesn't pause, swerving behind the screen wall into the courtyard. The last time he was here was over a year ago, when he spent a summer with his grandmother. He heard that Man's family has moved away.

In his recollection of that summer, all the adults ever did was sit on plastic stools in the courtyard and converse over cups of Longjing tea and bowls of roasted melon seeds. The children spent their weeks looking forward to every Friday, when they knew they'd find a box of mushrooms under the lion dogs in the morning. Bai Yu would fetch the box and Man would be in the kitchen – apron tied and hands washed – before anyone else. It was that summer when Bai Yu learned how to use a stove. They never found out who sent the mushrooms.

Past the second gate, the courtyard is empty. Because of his grandmother's sociable personality, Bai Yu expected to see two or three people at the very least. But there is no one there. After the sounds of people out on the streets preparing for the holiday, the silence in the courtyard is pure and cruel. He knows that what he hears is the quietness of a long-abandoned place.

'Nai Nai!' Bai Yu calls out.

His grandmother does not respond. Still panting, he wipes away the dust on the windowpane with one of his sleeves and peers into the main building, his breath fogging up the glass. His grandmother would never allow her house to get so dirty. The muted sunlight fails to illuminate anything inside, so he gives up and wiggles the doorknob. It isn't locked. He glances around to make sure that nobody has shown up. Before stepping inside, he remembers his bicycle in front of the gate and, fearing that somebody might take it after all, he runs to retrieve it. He breathes a sigh of relief upon finding that it's right where he left it. He raises the kick-stand, returns like the wind and leans the bicycle against the wall. He puts the box of mushrooms next to the bike, on the ground. He knocks on all the doors and waits patiently for someone to answer. After confirming that all the buildings are unoccupied, he slides into the main building.

As soon as he is inside, he questions whether he is in the right place. Everything he sees is covered in a fluorescent orange glow. He is glad to find that it is much warmer inside. Before trying to make sense of the strange sight, he wonders what has happened to his grandmother. Apart from that summer, he hasn't spent much time with the old woman. His father rarely speaks of her, since his uncle has assumed the responsibility of taking care of their mother. During the two months Bai Yu lived with his grandmother, she was admitted to the hospital four times. When that happened, in unspoken agreement, her sons made preparations for her death, each in their own way. Yet, time and time again, she recovered, like a dying tree that comes back to life every spring. To Bai Yu, it seemed as though she was living on willpower alone. He had never thought that human life could be so resilient.

But now she is gone. He can't quite explain this

feeling, but he knows that she isn't at the market or visiting the neighbours. He instinctively understands that
his grandmother hasn't moved away; that she is dead
and his father has concealed the news from him. Maybe
his father thinks that Bai Yu is too young to know about
death.

Bai Yu has always imagined that the death of a family
member would overwhelm him with emotions that he's
never experienced in his eleven short years of life. But
instead, he finds that the emptiness of the house carries
scarcely any weight inside him. For now, it is a place
that feels strange only because nobody is there.

Yet he does feel a throbbing sadness clenching his
heart. It isn't because his grandmother is gone from this
world, but because he will not be able to see her today.
When he wakes up tomorrow, this feeling will fade like a
star at dawn, but it will return one day, too bright to look
at. That day will come years later, during a stifling summer, when he will find himself back at this courtyard
letting out a loud, frenzied cry over what he has found
out today, as though he is learning it for the first time. He
will come to understand that a place can die with a
person.

He looks around him at the orange walls and floors.
Cautiously, he runs his fingers along the table and
chairs in the main room where he and his grandmother
used to have their meals together. Everything feels like
it is covered in a layer of rubber. He decides to check

the rooms, but the one to the left is locked. It is the one that connects to the other rooms, so there isn't much he can do. He calls his grandmother's name through the keyhole. He doesn't hear anything other than his own voice, which sounds as if it has been sealed in a container. He sits down and decides to wait for a while. Maybe somebody will come.

Just as he is having trouble deciding what to do, he hears music. He springs up and looks around. The sound of piano music is flowing from the locked room. Bai Yu presses his ear to the door and listens to the unfamiliar melody. He doesn't know what the piece is. It starts off with a blurry serenity, but as it continues it begins to take on a dark and terrifying clarity. He can tell that the mood of the piece is supposed to be fluid and calm, so he doesn't know why it sounds like it is about to tear through the door and eat him up.

He doesn't dare to move. His heart starts to beat faster than when he's riding his bike at full speed. He presses his hands over his chest. The orange walls seem to be shifting in all directions in front of his eyes – left and right, round and round. A flash of panic surges through his body. He can't take it any more. He runs out the door, through the gates, onto a bus and all the way home. He doesn't tell anyone about what happened.